SHATTERING GLASS

When the police find a dead girl — her jugular vein severed by the jagged top of a smashed bottle of eau-de-cologne lying nearby — their suspicion falls on her missing fiancé, Richard Lane. Later, when another girl is being followed by Lane, things look set for a second murder. But all is not as it seems, and it is not until the criminal psychiatrist Dr. Adam Castle takes a personal interest in the case that the bizarre facts are revealed.

JOHN RUSSELL FEARN

SHATTERING GLASS

Complete and Unabridged

LINFORD
Leicester

First published in Great Britain

First Linford Edition
published 2006

British Library CIP Data

Fearn, John Russell, *1908 – 1960*
    Shattering glass.—Large print ed.—
Linford mystery library
    1. Detective and mystery stories
    2. Large type books
    I. Title
    823.9'12 [F]

    ISBN 1–84617–226–8

Published by
F. A. Thorpe (Publishing)
Anstey, Leicestershire

Set by Words & Graphics Ltd.
Anstey, Leicestershire
Printed and bound in Great Britain by
T. J. International Ltd., Padstow, Cornwall

This book is printed on acid-free paper

1

Six years of war, and two decades of rebuilding and redevelopment, might have changed the face of London, but it had not changed the Bachelors' club. It was still as austere as it had been in 1939 — gray-fronted, stone-pillared, its heavy oak doors surmounted by the Gothic archway, which is the delight of the antiquarian and the despair of the modernist. It lay to the rear of what once had been prosperous residences and which now were nothing but rubble heaps — a squat, invincible building looming with a certain air of aloof complacency amidst a spider's web of alleys, small jewelers' shops, second-hand dealers and light industries. The glory that had been was no more; this disgusting element of commercialism had crept in and around the Bachelors' club, a product of the post-war era.

'Once,' Perry Lonsdale said pensively,

'I was actually content with all this — proud to consider myself a member of this august community. Surprising sometimes how one's views can change, isn't it?'

'I presume, sir,' the bartender said as he saw Perry Lonsdale looking with sour interest at the distant vision of gray and bald heads over the backs of chairs, 'you find it a bit — slow?'

'Slow!' Perry laughed shortly. 'Man alive, it's dead and doesn't know it! I can't think how I ever came to join as a member. Even less can I imagine why I was once perfectly satisfied with it all.'

Perry Lonsdale was tall and narrow when seen sideways, yet when seen from the front or back he was broad across the shoulders. Fair hair lay firmly brushed so as to accentuate a surprisingly high left temple, of which he was secretly extremely proud. The fingers holding the whiskey glass were sensitive; the sharp-featured face was smiling somewhat wryly. It was the expression of a man suffering from intense uncertainty engaged in the relentless struggle of trying to adjust his mind from the hectic life of a pilot to that of a very moneyed but diabolically lonely civvy street.

'I had the time of my life in the RAF,' he said, smiling half to himself. 'I've tried everything I can think of to squeeze a bit of juice out of life and all I've got is the pip. As for this place . . . '

He shook his head finished the drink and stood regarding the glass in his hand.

'How long have you been back in civvy street, sir?' the bartender inquired, folding a napkin swiftly and laying it neatly on one side.

'Six weeks. Long enough to realize that I'm sorry I left.'

'One thing has not changed . . . ' The bartender was solemn and profoundly sure of himself. 'I mean women. A woman might buck you up, sir.'

Perry Lonsdale grinned widely. 'I know girls by the truckload and they bore me completely . . . ' He sighed and shook his head again. 'No, I shall have to go abroad or something. Or I might even consider joining the Foreign Legion. Whatever happens, you won't see me in here again in a hurry, unless it's to be embalmed. I've got to do something — anything.'

Trailing vague conjectures behind him like a garment, Perry Lonsdale went across to the check clerk, took his hat and coat and donned them slowly because there was no conceivable reason why he should hurry. Nobody was waiting for him; nobody cared what in blazes he did. Finally, with a liberal tip and a languid nod, he stepped beyond the oak doors into the dark reek of the London night.

Suddenly the blur of sounds that made up this moment of 10.30 in London's nightlife was shattered by one savage and unmistakable noise — shattering glass. Perry Lonsdale turned his head sharply and finished buttoning his overcoat. The noise had come from somewhere on his left, somewhere in that dark, tangled jungle of second-hand dealers, jewelers and light industrial factories — all of which were closed.

A car appeared, moving at high speed. Its headlights blazed with a bewildering brilliance down a side street. They swung, rounded a corner, and shone full upon

Perry Lonsdale for a moment, and vanished as the big car roared away into the night.

Footfalls — suddenly. Swift, pattering, emphatic, coming nearer and nearer, running, filling the wide, deserted street with echo and re-echo. Perry Lonsdale finished his descent of the three steps of the Bachelors' club entrance and looked at the slender figure of the woman hurrying toward him. She was leaning slightly to one side, weighted down by a large suitcase. She glanced backwards and bumped clean into Perry.

'Oh!'

'Sorry,' Perry said, raising his hat. 'Very sorry. I hope I didn't hurt you?'

'No — no, of course you didn't. I'm all right . . . I suppose it was my own fault, really. Silly of me not to look where I was going.'

The girl turned to move on, but hesitated as the shrill blast of a constable's whistle smote the air.

'In trouble?' Perry asked quietly.

'No.' But the girl was breathing hard and it did not seem to be entirely from the exertion of running. 'You see, I — '

She did not finish her sentence. The gleaming cape of a constable loomed out of the night and a powerful torch blazed inquisitively. Perry Lonsdale glared.

'Confound it, officer, is your sight bad or what?' he inquired. 'Can't you see me — or rather us?'

'Sorry, sir.' The voice was gruff and the light was extinguished. 'Maybe you can help me . . . Seen anything of a smash-and-grab party round here tonight?'

The girl put down her heavy suitcase and the eyes of both the constable and Perry strayed to it. Then Perry looked up again.

'I did hear glass being smashed,' he confessed. 'Then I saw a big black closed car moving as though it were trying to beat the world's speed record. Came right past me on the road here and seemed to come from one of those alleys.'

'And you, miss?'

'I saw an attempted smash-and-grab.' The girl spoke without hesitation and seemed in full possession of her wits. 'In the lamplight I could see three men in

6

that car. One threw a brick or some sort of object as he jumped out of the car. Another man followed him. They dived for the window they'd broken. Then when they saw me watching they just made a hasty grab at the brick again, dived back to the car and drove off. I — I sort of got scared and started running — until I collided with this gentleman.'

'Perry Lonsdale,' Perry murmured, raising his hat again. 'Good evening.'

'I'm Moira Trent.'

Two more gleaming capes and helmets appeared from the distance. A squad car with its purple police sign on the roof, pulled up at the curb.

'Well, Miss Trent, that's all very interesting,' the constable said, finally, and it became apparent that amidst the folds of his cape he had been making notes under the lamplight. 'I'd like you — and you too, sir — to come along to the station and sign a statement. It will help us a lot.'

'Glad to,' Perry conceded, and after a brief pause Moira Trent nodded.

The officer opened the rear door of the

car. Perry heaved in the suitcase, then the girl and he settled themselves in the leather upholstery. The girl, Perry noticed, kept her hand on the suitcase.

'Nothing like the unexpected to brighten life up a bit,' he commented genially.

'That,' Moira Trent said, 'is what I don't like. I prefer things ordered and planned. Things that happen unexpectedly upset everything. It's like drying your face on a wet towel when you expect to find a warm one.'

The car pulled up in front of the station. Perry helped the girl out; then, seizing her case, he tugged it into the bare, barrack-like building.

'This won't take a moment,' the constable said. 'I'll just type out your statements and then you can sign them.'

The typewriter began clicking. Perry shifted his gaze a trifle and found Moira Trent looking at him.

'Not very talkative, are you?' Perry asked genially.

She gave a brief, troubled smile and glanced about her. Then she sighed. 'It's this place. A police station is no place to talk. Doesn't give you any inspiration.'

Finally the clicking of the typewriter ceased and the constable walked forward with two separate statements in duplicate and laid them on the counter.

'This is what each of you said,' he explained. 'If you'll just sign 'em and put your addresses . . . ' He took a pen from the rack and held it for the girl. She took it and wrote 'Moira Trent' with as many curves as a chorine. Perry scribbled his signature.

'That all?' he asked pleasantly.

'Er — not quite. I'd like to know your address, Miss — er — Trent?'

'I haven't got one yet,' she answered. 'I only arrived in London late this evening.'

'But you must be going somewhere?'

'I have a place in mind, certainly, but until I get there and can be sure of a room, I can't truthfully call it an address, can I?'

'Then where,' the constable asked, 'did you come from?'

A fraction's hesitation, then — 'Bristol.'

The red, freckled hand wrote 'Bristol'

and added in parenthesis — 'Of no fixed abode.'

'Confound it,' Perry objected, 'you make her sound like a tramp!'

'Sorry, sir, but in the legal sense that's what she is without an address. And there's something else, Miss Trent. I'd like to know what you've got in that bag . . . '

'Well, I — '

'I'll handle this.' Perry interrupted and to the constable he said calmly, 'You're exceeding your duty, officer. We are only witnesses, not suspects.'

'That, sir, I grant. But I am entitled to ask the young lady, and I'm doing it. It's merely to help. If you refuse, miss,' he told her, 'you'll be quite within your rights — but we can always take the necessary steps to get in touch with you, and the suitcase, should we wish.'

'Don't do it,' Perry instructed her but she only smiled slightly.

'It doesn't really matter.' With a quick movement she snapped open the lid. She waved a hand to it and said: 'Please don't embarrass me too much.'

The constable peered into the case. So did Perry. It was filled with lacy feminine trifles and at one end were half a dozen thick books, which evidently accounted for the weight. The constable pushed his hand in the miscellany of garments and stirred them slowly as though he were mixing a pudding. But he didn't miss a single corner. Then he picked up the books, examined them carefully, dropped them back into the case.

'Mmmm — all right,' he said finally and sounded most disappointed.

Perry picked up the suitcase and followed the girl out of the police station. The constable watched them go. Then he picked up the statements and went across to the private office. He knocked on the door and a bass voice responded.

At the desk in the center of the office sat Divisional Inspector Latham and the station inspector, a worried looking individual with thinning hair.

'Reports from the only witness and part-witness, sir,' the constable announced.

The divisional inspector looked at them and sighed.

'When we received your message — ' he looked at the constable — 'I thought we had a good chance of tracing the Farrish gang. That's why I took charge personally — but now it seems that I was wrong. The Farrish gang would never let a woman interfere with their plans. They'd have killed her first.'

'Then maybe the woman's lying sir,' the constable suggested.

'No, she wasn't lying,' Latham said. 'Before I came here I had Millington, the jeweler, visit the store and look over the stock. Nothing had been taken except the object used to smash the window, and that tallies with the girl's statement. Though why on earth the thieves took the trouble to retrieve the smasher and left thousands of pounds worth of jewelry behind is something I don't understand. The only damage apart from the window, was two cut-glass rose bowls smashed to bits. It's queer — infernally queer. It doesn't smell like the Farrish crowd to me.'

2

At the end of the little alley in which stood the police station, Perry Lonsdale and Moira Trent came to a stop.

'What,' Perry asked, pulling out his cigarette case 'happens now, Miss Trent?'

'I'd certainly like a meal,' she admitted slowly, 'and something hot to drink. But let it be somewhere quiet where we can sort of creep in and be left undisturbed.'

'I know of a place,' he said presently. 'Bill's Hash House. Best meal in London and only about a quarter of a mile from here. Come along.'

He could not be sure, but he fancied he saw a look of intense gratitude directed towards him. Picking up the suitcase, he took the girl's arm and they strolled down the main street.

'I never expected to run into a smash and-grab within my first few minutes of arriving in London,' Moira said.

'I never expected to be bumped into by

a running girl when I left the mortuary,'
Perry answered.

'Mortuary?'

'Sorry — Bachelors' club. Little difference. I'd show you what I mean only
you're the wrong sex — Say, are you a
bachelor girl?' he asked, in a sudden
kindling of anxiety.

'Yes I've no attachments at all . . . now.'

The last word left a hangover of
question marks in Perry's brain, but he
did not force the pace.

'No parents either?'

'No. They died in an accident when I
was very young. Until I was 18 I lived
with an aunt — then I went my own way.'

Silence again, save for their echoing
footfalls.

'You've been very kind to me, Mr.
Lonsdale,' the girl said presently, and
again there was that glance of gratitude.
'I'd like you to know that I really
appreciate it.'

Perry smiled. 'That's all right. Only too
glad. I'm just wondering about something, though. Funny how things come
back to you after a while. To where were

you running when you bumped into me?'

'I suppose,' the girl said, reflectively, 'it was a kind of panic. I simply wanted to get away from that spot. I'm like that in some things. Cool as can be when there is real danger, but when it's past I go to pieces.'

The little cafe was the only building in the quiet side street that had a lighted window. Perry opened the door and the girl preceded him into an aroma of warmth and food. A man of monstrous girth cast aside the evening paper and rose from behind a pile of cake stands.

'Well, well, if it isn't Mr. Lonsdale!' he exclaimed. 'I haven't seen you, sir, for — '

'Two years, Bill.' Perry told him genially, strolling across to the counter 'Seems like two centuries to me . . . Oh blast my manners! This is Miss Trent a friend of mine. Here we have Bill himself,' he said to the girl. 'The minister of the interior.'

The girl glanced around the empty dining room then, somewhat to Perry's wonderment, chose a distant partition-table farthest from the door.

'This,' she said, leaning back against the seat, 'is fine! Nobody peering at us, and we're unlikely to be disturbed . . . In fact, just the way I really like it. Don't you?'

'Immaterial.' Perry shrugged then glanced up as Bill arrived with two huge cups of steaming tea.

'Think they'll find the bottle-top murderer?' he asked. 'I was just reading about it.'

'The what?' Perry looked up in surprise.

'The bottle-top murder — or leastways that's what the papers are calling it.' He licked his lips in morbid glee. 'There's a really juicy crime for you! And you say you haven't read about it? A girl by the name of Joyce Kempton was murdered early this morning in Manchester. Somebody carved her so beautifully with the broken top of a bottle that it put paid to her jugular. Police inquiry is in full swing, I believe.'

'I haven't seen the paper,' said Perry, 'and if that's the main point of interest, I'm not sorry I didn't. Whoever she was, she probably deserved all she got.'

'No doubt,' Moira agreed, eating hungrily. 'And let me tell you something, Bill. The details don't go down very well with this supper.'

Bill started. 'Huh! I never thought of that — Sorry, miss. Sorry, sir.'

'What did you do in Bristol?' Perry asked presently. She answered without looking up.

'I was a stenographer, but the firm cut the staff down and I had to go. So I decided on London as the best place to look for a job. I suppose you have no conception of what it means to be out of work and practically broke.'

'Frankly,' Perry said morosely, 'I'm crawling with money and bored to death. Or rather, I was. You have sort of changed that.'

'I'm glad . . . though personally I think I must have been pretty much of a nuisance. After all, you didn't ask to have a strange girl wished on you in this fashion. Most men would have told me to keep my eyes open — after I bumped into you, I mean.'

'Well, that was the way it happened and

I regret nothing. How's the supper?'

'Perfect! And say, Mr. Lonsdale — '

'Oh, for heaven's sake, call me Perry. I just can't stick a lot of formality.'

'Perry, then.' She smiled. 'I was about to say that we'll have to part after supper. I've got to find a room, something that can't possibly interest you. We move in completely different orbits.'

'You're going to spend the night at the Barryvale hotel,' said Perry, 'and tomorrow we'll talk further on the matter.'

She looked at him for a moment and went on eating. Then she asked a question which was beginning to have a familiar ring.

'Is the Barryvale hotel quiet?'

'Fairly.' Perry frowned a little and considered her. 'Look here, Moira, what's this fetish you have for being quiet? Are you just naturally the retiring type or . . . or are you afraid of meeting somebody unpleasant?'

'It's just as I told you. I don't like a lot of company. I prefer to be alone. After all, that isn't unique, is it? Lots of people are like that.'

'Oh, sure they are — but they're mostly old ones. I can't imagine why a girl like you should want to hide herself.' Perry tried to read an answer in her expression, and failed. 'However, it's up to you. Suppose we change the subject? What sort of a job are you looking for?'

'Secretarial, same as before.'

'And you like the work?'

'Well, I have to live.'

Perry shook his head moodily. 'Yes, that's true enough, but of all the drab ways to do it I should say that making hieroglyphics and then typing them is about the worst. Look, Moira, suppose you had all the money you needed and could do as you pleased? What would you do?'

'Being only human, I'd enjoy it to the full . . . in a quiet way.'

'I knew that last bit would come up.' Perry grinned. 'You are a perfect living example of a rose wasting its sweetness on the desert air — Tell me about Bristol. Did you know many people there?'

'Oh, one or two. I — '

Moira stopped, her eyes fixed on the

steamy window. Perry glanced around and saw a man's face with soft hat pulled low over the eyes. Then it was gone.

'Do you mind if we leave?' she asked abruptly, and was on her feet before Perry answered.

'Leave? Because of — ?'

Perry dashed to the door, flung it open and stared into the street.

It was empty. Frowning. Perry closed the door. The girl was standing beside the table, apparently quite composed.

'What happened?' she asked.

'Happened?' Perry exploded. 'I was looking for the man who startled you . . . ' He came slowly towards the girl as he spoke. 'The one who looked through the window.'

'Honestly, Perry, I don't know what you're talking about. I only suggested we leave here because — well, we've finished supper, haven't we? And it's getting late.'

She turned to her suitcase, but Perry picked it up before she could grasp it. For the first time he noticed it had no initials.

'All right, we'll go,' he agreed. 'How much do I owe you, Bill?'

'Eight pounds, Mr. Lonsdale — And say, is there anything wrong?'

'Only with my head, I think.' With a grin Perry tossed a ten-pound note on the counter. 'All yours, Bill, and thanks for the feed. See you again some time.'

'You have a sublime disregard for risks, haven't you?' she asked after a while, and the look of gratitude was back on her face. 'You don't know a thing about me beyond the fact I'm from Bristol and that my parents are dead, yet you have taken on the job of being my guardian angel. How do you know I'm not a criminal, or somebody who might get you into a heap of trouble before you're finished?'

'How do you know I'm not?' he asked dryly. 'I might be a kid-glove killer, a lounge-suit blackmailer — or even that man, if man it was, who murdered the girl in Manchester with a bottle top . . . Never can tell. Your risk is as great as mine.'

'I'll take it,' she said at length.

'So will I. That makes us quits.'

It was 11.45 when they entered the Barryvale. To arrange for a room and see the girl safely to it did not take Perry above five minutes. Outside the door of Room 701 he stood regarding her.

'Tomorrow,' he said, 'we'll talk things over?'

'Tomorrow.' She nodded slowly, even happily. 'Shall we say 10 o'clock, in the lounge?'

'That'll suit me fine. I'll be waiting.'

3

Once within her room Moira Trent
locked the door and switched on the
light. She glanced at her suitcase, but
instead of opening it, began to unbutton
her overcoat.

'Naturally he saw me look at the cafe
window,' she said half aloud. 'He's no
fool. He knows it was because of that that
I decided to leave. I suppose I could have
been wrong, but I'm sure it was
. . . Dick.'

She turned restlessly and, crossing to
her suitcase, opened it and pulled out the
heavy books. One by one she put them on
the small table beside the bed. The titles
were varied, but they all covered the same
field — the mind. They ranged from a
cheap edition called *Master Yourself* to
Enrico Ferri's *Criminal Sociology*. Each
book was worn and thumbed.

The girl smiled as she glanced at them.
In the space of several years, she had read

each one from cover to cover.

'I know no more now than I did at first,' she mused. 'Either I'm completely dense or else there is no real answer — unless it be in the subconscious. And to understand that is like trying to pick the lock on the Bank of England.'

Climbing between the sheets, she lay gazing at the ceiling where the hole in the top of the lampshade traced a bright circle upon it. 'The bottle-top murder! The names they think of for sensationalism . . . '

★   ★   ★

When Perry Lonsdale arrived next morning he found a complete change had taken place in the shadowy, indifferently dressed woman he had befriended the previous night. The air of gloom and mysticism had gone. She was smiling and her red frock enhanced her features and, somehow, put a sparkle in her deep violet eyes.

'Well, well, and how is the bird of the night this morning?'

Perry sat down opposite her.

'I'm feeling very much as though I'm in wonderland, and still wondering how I'm going to repay you.'

'The first condition is understandable,' he said, 'and the second can be forgotten. I have a proposition for you. Not being a good salesman, I think I'd better start with a plush box and let that do the talking for me. That is, if you'll let it.'

Perry nodded and took a small case from his pocket. As he snapped it open Moira found herself staring at a massive diamond clawed on to a thin gold band.

'Why, it's beautiful! She inspected it closely. 'I don't think I have ever seen one quite so lovely. But,' — her eyes were deeply inquiring — 'why have you done this, Perry?'

'I think we should become engaged,' he said, trying to sound casual. 'To which I don't doubt that you will raise all sorts of objections about us not knowing much of each other. Let me make it clear that on my side that simply doesn't count. I'm the kind of chap who makes snap decisions. Up to now, all the women I've met — barring those in the forces who were usually engaged anyway — have been socialites, as shallow as soap-dishes and by no means as useful. It's different with you. I've thought about you most of the night and this morning I called on the jeweler. Now let's have your reaction.'

Moira sighed. 'What sort of a fool would I be to turn down a chance like this?' she murmured.

Perry smiled, took the ring and slipped it on the third finger of her left hand.

'You'll never regret this, Moira,' he said. 'I used to think that love-at-first-sight was sheer bunk; now I'm a convert. It can happen. In fact, it has. If there is anything I should know about you, I'm just not interested. As for me, my offerings include my money — more or less unlimited; my London flat, and my country home. Most important of all, I'm offering my love.'

'Country home?' Moira's unfathomable eyes brightened. 'Where? Near here?'

'You have mentioned,' Perry said mysteriously, 'that you like quiet places. My country place, the 'Larches,' is quiet,

26

even dull in some respects, but that can be changed with a woman's touch. It's in Somerset, on the borders of a little place called Brinhampton, near Taunton. I'd much prefer to live in London, but I expect that you — '

'I'd much prefer Somerset. I love the country — the peace and the quiet it brings.'

Perry beamed with joy. 'Leave everything to me,' he said. 'This is going to be a Lonsdale wedding, with all the pomp and glory that attaches to the name.'

'Well, I . . . ' Moira hesitated a long moment, then her hand with the gleaming diamond reached across the table. 'Of course, Perry. Whatever you say.'

'Fine!'

★ ★ ★

In one of the many offices at Scotland Yard, a conference was in progress.

'Frankly, sir, I can't make head or tail of it,' Division Inspector Jones of the Manchester C.I.D. said. 'I've followed every rule in the book and made every inquiry I can, but there still does not seem to have been any particular reason for the murder of Joyce Kempton. That's why I had all the information relayed to you. The facts are straightforward enough. Joyce Kempton roomed on Barbor Street. Quite an ordinary sort of place, same as any bachelor girl might have. She was a salesgirl at the perfume counter of Bagshaw's Emporium on Portland Street. She had no apparent enemies. She had a boy-friend named Richard Lane, but from what I can make out he kept company with a girl called Sylvia Cotswood as well.'

'Look here, Jones, I'm not a memory expert,' Chief Inspector Raymond Calthorp interjected. 'Stop reeling off all these confounded names, will you? It gets confusing . . . Let's get back to this chap Richard Lane. You have interviewed him, of course?'

'That's what I'd like to do, sir, but I can't. He's gone. I went to his rooms, but his landlady told me he'd left the evening before Joyce Kempton was found murdered. I've got McDane busy trying to trace him, but so far without result. I do consider it significant, though, that he told his landlady about 7 o'clock that he was going to spend the evening with Miss Kempton.'

'What sort of a statement has Miss Kempton's landlady got to make?' Calthorp asked musingly.

'She simply says she didn't see anybody strange about. It's one of those strictly ruled boarding-houses where young men are not permitted to visit girl boarders. On the other hand, it has an ever-open front door so the boarders can come and go without hindrance. Anybody could have entered, of course, but since the landlady occupied the front room and has her eyes on most of the things that go on, it doesn't seem likely. Only thing I can think of is the fire escape, which passes the window of Joyce Kempton's room.'

'I see. The girl had been lying dead all night, then?'

The divisional inspector nodded. 'According to the doctor she'd been dead 12 or 13 hours, which would be between 7 and 8 o'clock the previous evening. That casts suspicion on Richard Lane since he had planned to meet her at 7 o'clock. There'd been a struggle, too. That girl fought hard to save her life, I'd say — But you've seen the photographs of it?'

'I've seen them and studied them,' said the chief inspector, 'together with the reports from the forensic laboratory and fingerprint department. All forensic can tell us is that the girl was slain by the jagged top of a bottle. It severed the jugular vein and inflicted other severe injuries as well. The blood on the bottle-top checks with that of the girl. The bottle had contained eau-de-cologne.'

'That's right, sir,' the divisional inspector agreed. 'I discovered the bottle had come originally from the perfume counter in the emporium where the girl worked. She might have purchased it herself, but my guess is that Richard Lane bought it for her. Maybe he told her to select what she wanted from her own counter and then paid for it. Though why he should want to kill her afterwards is something which goes right beyond me.'

'I believe this bottle was empty?'

Calthorp inquired.

'After breakage it was, but there was eau-de-cologne beside the dressing table. In fact it was the aroma and the girl's silence that led her landlady to call the police. The door was locked on the inside, by the way, which again suggests the fire escape.'

Calthorp picked up the photograph of the bottle and studied it.

'And there are no fingerprints? No anything?'

'Nothing.' Even poroscopy doesn't tell us anything. As it looks right now, Joyce Kempton was murdered for no apparent reason — in the most homicidal manner possible.'

Chief Inspector Calthorp got up from his chair and sauntered over to the window. Without turning his head he said. 'What about this girl Sylvia Cotswood? Since she is Richard Lane's other girl friend, she's important. Have you interviewed her?'

'Not yet. I haven't found out where she lives. I learned from Joyce Kempton's associates at the emporium that Joyce had talked a lot about Lane, and mentioned several times that she considered herself far better than that 'frozen piece' Sylvia Cotswood to whom, it seems, Lane had been attracted before he took a sudden interest in Joyce.'

Calthorp glanced round. 'You mean to tell me Joyce was prepared to stand for that sort of thing — ? To share Lane with this other girl?'

'I hardly think it was that,' Jones replied. 'I believe that Joyce was determined to prove that she was a better bet than Sylvia, more in the spirit of good-natured rivalry than anything else. That isn't an uncommon thing in love affairs, sir. Two men often love the same girl and are willing to let her make the choice. I think that is what happened in this case, except the positions were reversed. Two girls and one man.'

'Mmm — maybe,' Calthorp agreed. 'She must have been a girl of uncommon broad-mindedness. It is not the usual thing to find a woman willing to permit another woman in what she considers is her exclusive territory. However, it could happen, I grant you. And you couldn't find out any more concerning Sylvia Cotswood?'

'No. Of course, Joyce had never mentioned Sylvia's address, or even if she lived in the same city. I'd hoped to get that from Richard Lane, but now I'm at a dead end.'

4

From the moment she had the diamond engagement ring placed on her finger, Moira had been constantly on the go. Ignoring her pleas that she preferred solitude, Perry took her first to his London flat, where she met Pearson, the only existing member of the Lonsdale domestic staff, and then on to Brinhampton and the 'Larches.' Pearson, who also acted as chauffeur, drove while Perry and the girl sat back and enjoyed the scenery.

'I seem to be living in a dream,' Moira said, closing her eyes. 'Everything happens so efficiently — and you pour out money as though it's water. I've bought everything I ever thought of or even dreamed about.'

'Including your trousseau,' Perry reminded her. 'My part in the wedding business is a special license. We're going to be married on Friday, exactly a week after our engagement. That's a bit more of the efficiency you were talking about.'

'On Friday!' Moira opened her eyes in surprise. 'But I thought you said it was going to be marriage on the grand Lonsdale style? I've had visions of church bells, cheering spectators throwing confetti, dozens of your friends, the organ booming mightily — '

'None of which you really care about,' he pointed out.

'Well no, but if it pleases you . . . '

'I thought better of it. After all, these are austere days. With this special license we can be married anywhere in the country, so why not at the Larches? Just the minister, a few friends. No more than four with two of them as witnesses. I've already written them. You'll make their acquaintance when we get home — home being the Larches from now on. They're turning up for a house-warming and, of course, will be with us until after the ceremony.'

Moira nodded slowly, a somewhat wondering, bothered look crossing her face.

'And after we're married?' she inquired.

'Where do we honeymoon?'

'The south of France. Be a bit warmer. I've made reservations so there's nothing to worry about.'

'It will be wonderful, Perry — and you've planned everything so marvelously — but didn't you say that you have no staff at the Larches? That Pearson is the only man you've been able to get hold of so far?'

'Pearson was down here yesterday engaging a new staff. Matter of fact he's only been with me six weeks or so. Nothing has been overlooked. You'll see.'

Moira made no more observations on the subject, content with his assurance all would be well. Towards late afternoon they drew near a massive 18th-century type manor house. Moira watched as they approached it and her breathing quickened.

'You mean you own that? That I'll be the mistress of it?' she asked Perry eagerly.

'If it appeals to you. If it doesn't I can very soon buy another one.'

'Appeals to me!' she gasped. 'Why, I

have never seen anything so marvelous. It looks to me like something out of fairyland! I've not been used to such wonderful things.'

'Then don't ever say so out loud,' he said, with gentle firmness. 'I shall want my wife to act as to the manor born — and no pun intended. Now, get yourself ready — the folks will be waiting for us.'

They were. Two young men and women came speeding down the broad steps and wrenched open the car doors. Moira recoiled a little as grinning faces studied her critically.

'Have a heart!' Perry protested. Give the girl a chance to get to know you — '

'Nothing doing, Perry,' one of them told him calmly. 'First impressions are the most important. Mmmn — so you finally managed it! Didn't make any mistake in your choice, either — eh, Dick?'

Both stood at mock attention as Moira stepped out of the car. She gave a quick glance about her and almost immediately found herself seized by the two young women.

One was blonde, dumpy, and laughing; the other tall and dark, not unlike Moira herself. Laughing protestingly, Moira was swept into the great hall.

Here she paused breathlessly and turned as Perry came in with the two young men hanging upon his arms.

'Well,' said the one who had appraised Moira, 'you wanted the house warmed and a cheerful welcome on the mat. You got it. Now what happens?'

'You don't have to be so confoundedly wholesale,' Perry objected. 'Moira hates this kind of thing. She much prefers things quiet and secluded.'

'That,' said the young man solemnly, 'is positively morbid. In fact it is a condition which must be outgrown — and quickly.'

'Take no notice of 'em,' Perry smiled, taking Moira's arm and drawing her to him. 'And while I'm about it, let me clear up the identities of this crazy quartet. This chap with the yellow hair and vacant expression is Dick Mills, one of the best navigators the RAF ever had, and also my best friend.'

'Grand knowing you, Moira,' grinned

the young man. 'Perry walked off with the prize after all — and that,' he added soothingly as his blonde companion gave him a sharp look, 'isn't meant to slight you, Betty darling. In any case, you are my type — honey-haired. So don't start thinking things.'

'This,' Perry went on, 'is Dick's wife — Betty.'

'Take no notice of Dick,' Betty said cheerfully. 'He's always clowning. I've been married to him for five years and am sort of used to it.'

Moira smiled and shook the hand held out to her. 'I'm sure you're both happy people,' she said.

'And here's Helen Ransome,' Parry said, as the dark-headed girl moved forward. 'And Will Ransome — brother, not husband.'

'Nice knowing you, Moira,' said the young man.

'Very nice,' Helen agreed. 'And don't mind me staring at you a little, Moira, will you? I've been trying to think of whom you remind me.'

'I?' Moira gave a little start. 'Why who is it?'

'Myself,' Helen decided, shrugging. 'We look enough alike to be sisters. Same dark hair, same height, same build. I'm sure we must have a lot in common.'

'I hope I shall have a lot in common with all Perry's friends,' Moira replied.

'Tell you what you do,' Perry said, catching Moira's arm. 'Just get acquainted while I see how Pearson has fixed up the domestics.'

'Better still,' Helen Ransome said, 'I'll show you to your room — then we can go over the place if you like. I know every corner of it. When Perry and I were children we used to play here a lot . . . Come along.'

Moira nodded as Helen took her arm and together they went towards the massive staircase.

'This business seems so sudden,' Helen said, as they ascended. 'Or rather unexpected. Nothing to do with me, of course, and please don't think I'm trying to be inquisitive, but how on earth did you manage to hook him?'

'We met by accident,' Moira responded, in no mood to give full details. 'It wasn't that I fell for him so much as he fell for me.'

'Then I don't understand it,' Helen sighed.

'Don't understand what?'

They had come to the head of the great staircase. Helen pointed along the corridor with its towering, stained-glass windows.

'Your room's along here,' she said. 'I've spent quite a bit of time telling the housekeeper what to do. Perry relies implicitly on my judgment, you know.'

'I didn't know.' Moira reflected briefly. 'What is it that you don't understand?' she asked. 'You were saying — ?'

'Oh, that!' Helen Ransome gave a serious little smile. 'I don't understand what it is that you've got and I haven't. We are alike in appearance, and I've tried my level best to get Perry to marry me — but to no avail. Then he chooses you! The only answer I can think of is that you have some kind of hypnotic power. There can't be any other reason, can there?'

'Except that we love each other,' Moira suggested coolly.

'Doesn't count for much these days,' Helen said. 'Anyway, Perry marrying you shows you can never tell with men — and they say it's the women who provide the unpredictable element! I shan't believe that any more. Well, here's the room you will be using until after the wedding.'

'It's beautiful,' Moira observed.

'Best room in the house,' Helen sighed. 'Of its size, that is. I used to have it when I came over to stay: now I'm pushed into a smaller one. All according to Perry's special orders. I suppose I can label myself his forgotten woman — '

'Why don't you go and sharpen your claws on some other tree, Helen?'

Perry's easy voice inquired, and both women turned to see him lounging in the corridor, shoulder against the door jamb. As he met their gaze he came forward and put a protective arm about Moira's shoulders. 'Helen been baring her fangs at you?' he asked, smiling.

'Well, of course I have,' Helen admitted, raising an eyebrow. 'You don't expect me to accept defeat with gracious charm, do you? In my opinion, the woman who'll do that isn't yet born. Well, I think I'll leave you two to finish the tour by yourselves. See you again, Moira, and don't think too badly of me. I have the darnedest habit of saying just what I think.'

She turned languidly and ambled down the corridor.

'Very outspoken,' Moira commented.

'I shouldn't have left you alone with her,' Perry apologized. 'It never occurred to me that she might let herself go. Habit she's got. The rest of us are used to it and shut her up accordingly, but strangers don't always understand. She's harmless enough, but a bit piqued, I think, because I've never asked her to marry me.'

'You chose me, Perry, and I'm not much different.'

'The difference lies in the fact that I love you and I don't love her. I don't have to enlarge on that, do I?'

'No, of course not.' Moira walked over to the window. For a while she studied the wintry grounds. March was a long time shaking off his frosty garments this year. 'How about the servants?' she inquired presently. 'Did Pearson fix it up?'

'As well as he could under present conditions. All we have is a cook-housekeeper and Pearson himself. The best we can do until the agency sends us some maids. We'll get by. I have an idea, somehow, that you're the managing sort.'

Moira did not reply. She was gazing beyond the grounds at the dimly rising mists of evening. Perry studied her for a moment, then went over to her. To his surprise there were tears in her eyes as she turned to face him.

'Crying?' he asked, amazed. 'What in the world is there to cry about? Something I've said — or done?'

'Of course not, Perry.' She made an effort to smile and rested a hand on his arm. 'You're the sweetest, gentlest man I have ever met. I was just thinking how awful it would be if I were to lose all this. There's such peace and contentment here. I can feel it. It's like a backwater, secure from the storm.'

'What storm?' he demanded, bewildered; then his voice firmed, suddenly.

'Moira, isn't it about time you put pretence aside and admit you fear something? I haven't forgotten how you behaved in the cafe that first night.'

She was silent, but her tears ebbed slowly. Perry waited, then shrugged.

'All right, you're entitled to have your secrets — but I think I should tell you that's one reason why I decided to marry you so quickly.'

Moira looked at him sharply, puzzled. 'Why? How do you mean?'

'I like danger,' he explained, grinning. 'To marry an ordinary humdrum woman would be too tame. That's why I never have married. With you there's none of that. There's some mystery about you, and I like it. You're afraid of somebody — and I think it's a man in a soft hat — but I like that, too. Because of our marriage I'll be able to share whatever danger may threaten you, and enjoy it; and I'll be able to protect you. Money and influence can do a lot.'

5

To Moira the few intervening days before her marriage passed so swiftly that she hardly noticed them. So the morning of the wedding inevitably came. The organist from Brinhampton village church played the wedding march on the grand piano, Betty Mills and her husband supplied the flowers. After the ceremony came the signing of the register — and the business was all over.

On the great desk in the center of the room were laid the offerings of countless friends from near and far. Helen surveyed them with her dark head on one side.

'I've looked through most of them — glanced, that is,' she said 'It's a funny thing but everything seems to be from somebody you know, Perry. As for you, Moira, nobody seems to care whether you've married or not. I don't see a single thing addressed to you personally.'

'As if it mattered,' Perry retorted.

'Everything here is intended for both of us, only you naturally would try to read something else into it. It's just that Moira has very few friends who know her movements.'

'Oh, I see.'

Helen exchanged a glance with Betty Mills. Will Ransome looked at Dick Mills. Moira said nothing. She was studying the various gifts, among which were two heavy cut-glass decanters. Round the neck of one was a card that read: *To Perry: Better to have loved and lost. Helen.*

'Thanks for the thought Hel,' Perry grinned, as Moira pointed it out to him. 'Do you expect me to drink myself to death?'

'Why not?' Helen suggested. 'It's about the best thing I can wish for you since I can't have you myself'.

'I have the idea,' said Betty Mills, 'that Helen doesn't much care for this marriage. It's stroked her the wrong way.'

'That I am afraid, is purely her own affair,' Perry replied indifferently. 'And I don't think we need attach all that importance to what she says. We all know Hel: too outspoken for her own good, sometimes. Anyway,' he added, 'let's have the wedding feast and then, my sweet, we've got to catch a train and boat for France.'

Moira nodded and accompanied him from the library. As she sat down at the dining table, Perry noticed her expression was curiously waxen and she scarcely noticed him; her thoughts were far away. She hardly heard the toast that Will Ransome proposed to the happy couple. She only seemed to become conscious of her surroundings when Perry placed a glass of champagne before her.

'To ourselves, sweetheart,' he murmured, bending over her. 'Didn't you hear what Will said?'

Moira hesitated, then suddenly jumped up and put a hand to her forehead.

'No, I — I didn't hear,' she said falteringly. 'And — and I won't drink either!' She glanced around at the startled assembly. 'I hate champagne! I hate this stuff on the table! I hate all of you staring at me — !'

She wheeled and without another word, strode from the dining room.

Will Ransome sat down slowly and stared like a man who has seen a miracle.

'Well, I'll be thrice darned!' he burst out. 'Say, what did we do?'

Perry rushed upstairs to the bedroom the girl had been using. He tapped lightly on the door and entered. Moira was standing by the window hastily drying her eyes with a handkerchief.

'Dearest, what on earth's the matter? What's gone wrong?'

'I — I know my behavior was unforgivable,' Moira whispered. 'It's my nerves, I suppose. I've been under a big strain . . .'

'Strain? But good heavens, this should be the happiest morning of your life!' He caught her shoulders and forced her to look at him. 'Moira, what is it? Downstairs you behaved just as you did in that cafe — abruptly, as though driven by a sort of impulse.'

'I often behave like that,' she said quietly. 'All I ask is that you'll forgive me . . . Look, Perry, would you care very much if we didn't go to France? I'm not at all keen on it, really.'

'But it's to be our honeymoon! Hang it all, Moira, you're simply tearing things up by the roots — '

'It doesn't have to be the south of France for our honeymoon.'

'We—ll, no, I suppose not, but everything's fixed up.' Perry gave her a worried look then sighed. 'All right, call it off. I'll reserve a suite at Claridge's instead.'

'I'd rather we had our honeymoon here, dearest. I just don't want to go away! Can't I impress that point on you? I love this place; it's so secure and peaceful.'

He smiled and patted her hand gently.

'All right, sweetheart, if that's the way you want it. I knew I was marrying a girl with strange tastes, so I suppose it serves me right. Here we are — and we'll stay. Now come downstairs again and let the folk see you. They just can't understand your behavior.'

Perry opened the door for her and she preceded him along the corridor. He caught up with her as they reached the stairs. When they entered the dining-room, conversation ceased and inquiring eyes turned to Moira.

'I owe each one of you, and Perry in particular, a profound apology,' she said quietly. 'I had no right to behave as I did. I can only say that it was a sudden attack of nerves. As I've told Perry, I'm affected that way sometimes.'

'You're sure you're all right now?' Betty Mills inquired. 'You don't feel ill or anything?'

'No, Betty, my health's all right, thanks — but I certainly don't feel up to going away. Perry has agreed that we'll honey-moon here, and just so as things won't get too dull, for Perry anyway, I want all of you to stay for, say a week.

'Of all the extraordinary ideas!' declared Will Ransome. 'Can't say when I've ever heard of anything like it!'

'It's certainly original,' Helen commented. 'The thing that amazes me is that you should want me to stay. I haven't been particularly pleasant towards you, Moira . . . ' She gave a slow, cynical smile.

'It's not that I'm apologizing; I'm just pointing it out.'

'I can understand your feelings and that's why I'm not resentful,' Moira replied. 'I'd probably feel the same if after years of struggle to get the man I wanted I discovered a stranger had walked in and taken him. I don't hold it against you.'

'Thanks,' Helen said, still looking vaguely astonished. 'Now that's settled I suppose we can consider ourselves one big, happy family?'

'We'll stay over, of course,' Betty said.

Perry tried to enliven things with dancing in the ballroom to radio and piano. Moira danced divinely, whether it was with him, Dick Mills or Will Ransome, but it was purely mechanical. Her mind was elsewhere.

They adjourned to the drawing-room around 10 o'clock.

'Of all the crazy set-ups this is about the craziest,' Helen murmured, just loud enough for Perry to hear. 'For goodness sake, Perry, give me a cigarette before I burst out weeping!'

Perry handed her his cigarette case and

she selected one.

'Look, Perry, are you sure you did the right thing?' she asked anxiously. 'Did you ever see such a line-up for a wedding night? Since we came from the ballroom everything has just died on its feet. Betty and her hubby playing cards, and that fat-headed brother of mine drawing sketches, and me racking my brains trying to think of something original and amusing. As for your wife . . . '

Perry shifted position uncomfortably and shied away from Helen's suddenly questioning gaze. He knew her well enough to realize that her emotions were not really as brutal as her words implied. Helen Ransome had the unfortunate drawback of seeming downright vicious, until one managed to discover that she had a welling generosity somewhere deep inside.

'I'll admit,' he said moodily, glancing over at Moira, 'that I didn't expect it was going to be like this. It's disturbing, to say the least.'

'You've never told me yet why you did decide to marry her. Quite all right if you don't want to, of course, but I'm not exactly a stranger. Hang it all, Perry, I can give you everything any woman can — and a darned sight more than this broody hen you've picked . . . What started it? I'm interested.'

'I don't quite know . . . She seemed exciting.'

'Exciting!' Helen stared blankly. 'Moira?'

'Well then, mystifying,' Perry amended. 'I was just feeling thoroughly browned off with everything and everybody in general when she came running out of the night and bumped into me. Then . . . ' He sketched in the finer points of this experience, his voice low, and in the end smiled a little whimsically. 'So, feeling attracted to her, chiefly because of the apparent element of danger and the fact she needed protection, I decided to marry her.'

'Then,' Helen said, wondering, 'you don't really know anything about her? She just came out of the night and, when everything's boiled down, you've taken her on trust?'

'I don't know any more than she's told

me. Her parents are dead; she worked in Bristol as a secretary; they cut the staff down and — '

'Just about the crazy sort of thing you would do,' Helen interrupted.

6

Perry waited as Moira got up from her chair and came across the room. The look of despondency had gone. She was half smiling as though a particularly happy thought had occurred to her.

'Discussing me?' she inquired, looking down at Helen.

'As a matter of fact, yes,' Helen said. 'I was just remarking that for a bride a few hours old, you can surely do better than sit staring into the fire.'

Perry cleared his throat and raised his voice for all to hear.

'Hey, folks, how about some table tennis — or something?'

'I was thinking,' Moira said, 'that it might be more fun to go for a night ride in the cars — '

'Now there you've really got something!' Perry enthused, his eyes brightening. 'The very ticket!'

'I'll see what sort of a night we've got,'

Moira added. She stepped over to the window and parted the drapes.

'Any good?' Perry asked.

'Yes, it seems to be all — '

Moira stopped dead. In that split second Perry realized that he had heard her do that once before — in the cafe when she had seen a man looking through the window. He rushed to her side and with a little sigh, she collapsed in his arms.

'Fetch some brandy,' Perry directed. 'I'll take her upstairs. You chaps take a look outside and see if you can see anybody.'

'Okay,' Dick and Will chimed, and dived for the French window.

Frowning to herself, Helen went to the cocktail cabinet and poured some brandy. Betty Mills drifted over and their eyes met.

'If you want to know what I think — ' Betty began, but Helen cut her short.

'I don't. I can form my own opinion. That girl's plain crazy — or else artful.'

'No,' Betty said, shaking her head. 'I think you're wrong. My guess is that she's ill — very ill, but she just won't admit it.

Some people are like that; too much spirit for their own good, I say. Maybe she's been through a terribly tough time somewhere and won't speak about it.'

'And maybe not,' Helen said. 'What I want to know is: What made her faint?'

She picked up the glass of brandy and went up to the great chamber which Perry and Moira were using as their bridal suite. She found Moira on the bed, Perry bending over her and chafing her wrists. The bedside lamp shone upon the girl's still, pale face.

'How is she?' Helen asked.

'Still unconscious. I think we'd better get a doctor — '

Perry stopped talking as Moira stirred uneasily. He put an arm behind her shoulders, raised her head so that he could force the brandy between her lips. She gasped and choked, then opened her eyes.

'I — I fainted, didn't I?' she asked.

'Yes.' Perry patted her hand and glanced at Helen. 'Give Dr. Burridge a ring and ask him to come over right away. He'll be able to — '

'No, don't do that!' Moira's voice had acquired sudden strength. 'I'm all right, really — soon will be, anyway. I — I should have told you, Perry. I'm subject to these fainting spells. I didn't say anything because I . . . I didn't want you to think me weak.'

Helen picked up the empty brandy glass and left the room silently. Perry sat down on the bed beside Moira.

'Look here, dearest, don't you think it's time you gave me all the facts? So far I've let you keep your secrets to yourself, but we're married now. To say the least, your behavior is peculiar. The others are going to start talking — and we can't blame them. I want to be in the position to keep them quiet.'

'I couldn't help fainting, could I?' Moira asked, with sudden peevishness.

'I suppose not, but why did you faint? Was it because of something you saw outside the window?'

Moira hesitated before replying.

'Yes,' she said quietly. 'That was the reason.'

'What was it you saw outside the

window? The same thing — or person — you saw outside the cafe?'

'Yes.'

'But who is he?' Perry demanded. 'What does he want with you? Let's thrash this out and get rid of it! I can't stand much more of this mystery.' He caught Moira's shoulders and shook her gently. 'You've got to tell me, dearest; I insist.'

'I — I can't, Perry. Please I beg of you, don't ask me to explain.'

Moira stared at him dumbly, her eyes full of an expression he could not interpret. He released her abruptly and got to his feet.

'To advise the police is the only sensible course,' he said.

'But, Perry — '

There was a knock on the door. Perry turned impatiently.

'Yes, come in . . . '

It was Betty Mills who entered.

'I've been helping Dick and Will search the grounds,' she said. 'There's no sign of anything or anyone.'

Perry pursed his lips. 'All right, Betty, it

was just a whim of mine.'

'It must have been,' she affirmed. 'There are no footprints, either. How are you, Moira?'

'Oh, better, thanks.'

'I'm so glad . . . ' Betty hesitated. 'Well, that's all, Perry. I'd better go.'

Perry glanced at the closed door, then turned back to Moira.

'In most things, dearest, I'm more or less happy-go-lucky. I like a spot of excitement here and there . . . ' He sounded as though he were reciting a monologue. 'But things have got beyond that stage now, and I want action. I'm going to telephone for the police, and since you don't want to tell me anything, we'll see what the man himself has to say. The police will find him quickly enough.'

'But what are you going to tell them?' Moira asked. 'That I saw a man looking at me through the window and fainted because of it? How can you substantiate it? There are no footprints to prove it, nobody else saw him, and if I denied that I ever did see him — What then?'

'You mean you'd let me make a fool of

myself?' he asked brusquely.

'If you insist on telling the police, I will have no other course. All I want you to do is trust me. Trust me in just the same way as you've trusted me up to now. Please promise me you'll do that. I'll explain everything when I'm ready.'

Perry rubbed the back of his head doubtfully.

'All things considered, you leave me little choice! There is one thing you should do, though, and that's see a doctor. Maybe you're suffering from extreme nerves — hallucinations or something.'

Then suddenly he remembered that he, too, had seen somebody through the steamy window of Bill's Hash House. And something else occurred to him. He looked at Moira wonderingly.

'But, when we were in the cafe you denied seeing anybody,' he remarked slowly. 'Yet now you calmly admit it.'

'All right, maybe I didn't tell the truth. I didn't know you very well then. Certainly I didn't know that our lives were destined to become so interwoven.'

'I'd like to believe that that is the real explanation. Anyway, about calling the doctor — '

Moira's dark head shook stubbornly. 'I don't want a doctor, and if you call one I shall refuse to see him. I'm all right, and I know what I'm doing. I'll be a lot better after a good rest ... I'm not going downstairs again tonight.'

She stretched out her hand to Perry, and he could not ignore the beseeching look in her eyes.

'Please, Perry, don't think too badly of me. Can't we forget the whole thing for a while? Suppose you bring up some coffee for both of us and we'll sit and talk. Make some excuse downstairs. They'll manage all right — especially if Helen takes command.'

Perry hesitated, then nodded slowly.

'Coffee, eh? All right, I'll see to it.'

'For both of us, don't forget! I feel self-conscious when I drink alone.'

The moment he had gone, Moira slid from the bed, changed hurriedly into pyjamas and robe and then slipped back under the sheets. By the time Perry had returned with the coffee on a silver tray she was sitting up and looking remarkably composed.

'Changed in the interval, eh?' he said. 'Quick work! Glad to find you are feeling that much better.'

He sounded as though he did not know whether he ought to be surprised or not. He set the tray down on the bedside table and Moira poured two cups.

'What did you tell them down below?' she asked.

'I told them to do whatever they like — that neither of us would be seeing them until tomorrow morning. And I didn't phone for a doctor, either. I'm trusting you, Moira, as you asked me to, but I don't say how long that trust will endure. There's a limit to patience sometimes.'

'Yes . . . ' Moira stirred her coffee and smiled reflectively. 'Yes, isn't there?'

7

The unexpected events of the evening had completely damped the ardor of those left in the drawing-room below. Betty and her husband drifted back to their card game and Will Ransome resumed his sketching. Helen stood beside the fireplace for a long time, smoking a cigarette with a certain air of elegance. Finally she glanced at her watch. It was 11.45.

'I think I'll turn in,' she announced. 'With you two absorbed in those confounded cards and Will here monkeying with sketches, I'm the odd one out. See you in the morning — and let's hope our hostess behaves a little more rationally.'

The house grew quiet. Helen, lying in her bed, felt her senses drifting. Then she became aware of stealthy sounds. At first it was something being drawn softly across the carpet. Then it changed to a gentle but emphatic click.

65

Helen opened her eyes and peered into the darkness. Sheer laziness told her to go to sleep again, but her instinct warned her something was wrong. That there was deadly danger.

She reached out her arm to turn on the lamp, but the room remained dark. Someone was holding her wrist in a grip of steel.

'Who — who is it?' she demanded. 'Who — ?'

She gasped with pain as a stinging blow landed on her face. This was just the kind of punishment that set the venom boiling in her vigorous, downright nature. She was no longer frightened, just blazing mad. She flung the sheets at the shadowy figure. With frantic energy, she covered the head and shoulders, then scrambling out of the bed, she tugged and pulled with all her strength. But her foot caught in the trailing sheets and she sprawled on the floor. Her hand struck the bedlamp and sent it flying. There was a dull thud as the table fell over.

Helen staggered to her feet. A dim shadow fled across the room. The door opened and shut. Dizzily, she groped round for the bedlamp, and presently found it. She righted the table and stood the lamp upon it.

There was a knock on the door. Helen wheeled in alarm, then heaved a sigh of relief. It was Betty and Dick Mills.

'What's happened? What was all the noise?' Betty asked.

'That,' Helen replied grimly, 'is what I mean to find out. Did you see anybody in the corridor?'

'See anybody?' Betty gave her husband a quick glance. 'Why, no.'

Without another word, Helen slipped into dressing gown and slippers and hurried down the hall to the next room.

'Perry! Moira! Wake up!'

There was no response. She pounded on the door. No answer. So she turned the knob and stepped inside and turned on the light.

Perry and Moira were sound asleep. Helen frowned and went over to the bed slowly. Seizing Perry's shoulder she shook him fiercely, but he did not awaken. She tried the same tactics with Moira, and with far less ceremony, but the girl only sighed and slumbered on.

Her brother raised Perry's right eyelid.

'I'm no doctor,' he said, 'but I do know that any normal sleeping person would waken under that sort of treatment. It does seem as though they're drugged all right — Hello, what's this?'

He nodded to the tray on the bedside table with the empty coffee cups.

'The coffee Perry brought up,' Helen said. 'Remember he said he was going to? Don't touch those cups,' she added sharply. 'The police will want to see them.'

'The police!' Her brother stared at her. 'But why? Nobody's been hurt, have they?'

'Somebody attacked me tonight,' Helen informed him. 'I don't know why, or whether murder was intended. I was too quick for whoever it was.'

'Somebody tried — to attack you?' Will Ransome sounded incredulous.

'That's what I said, and whoever it was has either hidden in the house or else by this time has escaped so completely that we've no chance of following. Nip down and ring for the police, Will. I'm going back to my room to dress.'

Her brother nodded and hurried off and the others returned to Helen's room.

Recalling that she had heard cloth tearing during the scuffle, Helen picked up the sheets.

Then she gave a start. Something was lying on the floor, gleaming in the light. Betty and Dick looked also, but none of them touched it — the top half of a cut-glass decanter.

'Great Scot!' Dick Mills gasped. 'You were attacked with that!'

Helen laughed nervously.

'Evidently! I didn't know. It was so dark — Thank goodness I didn't.'

'It looks like the top of one of the decanters you gave Perry for a wedding present,' Betty said.

'That's exactly what it is,' Helen agreed. 'And don't touch it,' she cautioned. It may be valuable to the police. They keep things like this for fingerprints. You'd better rouse Pearson and Mrs. Carter. I expect the police will want to

69

question them, too.'

'I'll do that,' Dick promised.

Helen closed the door after them and paused as she turned the key in the lock. She remembered now that she had not locked it before. The necessity of doing so had not occurred to her.

Hastily she began dressing. She noted it was 2.30 a.m., an unearthly hour. Her brother knocked on the door to tell her the police were on their way — then 10 minutes later, her hair hastily arranged and clothes by no means as elegantly draped as usual, she went down to the drawing-room.

After a while she was joined by her brother, then came Betty and her husband. The domestics were the last to arrive. A thunderous hammering on the front door heralded the arrival of the police.

A square-faced inspector and tall sergeant came into the drawing-room, while a constable remained in the hall.

'Good evening, inspector — or rather morning,' Helen said. 'Sorry to have to drag you out like this.'

Inspector Chanworthy took off his cap and laid it on a chair.

'To some purpose, I hope,' he said irritably. 'What's wrong, Miss Ransome?'

He knew the girl well — as she did him. There had been times when he had exerted his officialdom and warned her about exceeding the speed limit in her roadster.

'All I know is that somebody attacked me tonight while I was in bed,' she said. 'I've not the vaguest idea who it was, or where that person is now — but the weapon is lying in my room.'

'Ah, good! You haven't touched it?'

'No.'

'I take it that nobody was hurt?'

'As it happens, no,' Helen replied, 'but I'm convinced it was an attack on my life.'

The inspector nodded, then glanced at the rest of the assembly. 'Good evening, Mr. Ransome,' he said pleasantly. 'Oh, and Mr. and Mrs. Mills! How are you — ?' His eyes passed over Pearson and Mrs. Carter as obvious domestics, then came back to Helen. 'But isn't this Mr. Lonsdale's house?' he asked.

'Mr. and Mrs. Lonsdale's house,' Helen corrected. 'He was married yesterday morning.'

'Ah, of course! I remember the announcement in the paper. They're away on their honeymoon?'

'No,' Will Ransome said. 'At the present they're upstairs in bed, apparently drugged or something. Sleeping as though dead.'

'Very strange,' Inspector Chanworthy observed. 'Anyway, Miss Ransome, let me see your room. Sergeant, you take Roberts and have a look round outside.'

'Right, sir.'

Chanworthy studied the jagged glass thoughtfully. Then he glanced at the torn sheets.

'Nasty weapon,' he observed grimly. 'What is it? The top of a decanter?'

'I think it is one of twin decanters I gave Mr. Lonsdale for a wedding present,' Helen replied. 'We can soon check on that by looking in the library. The presents haven't been moved far as I know.'

'Mmmm, I see.'

With the decanter perched on his hand like a glittering boxing glove, the inspector wandered about the room, peering here, brooding there. After a while he came to the window and drew back the drapes. The catch was firmly bolted.

'Now tell me exactly what happened, in detail,' the inspector said.

'I don't see any stopper to this,' he said, when the narration was over. 'Should be one. We'd better look for it.'

They all joined in the search but were unsuccessful. The inspector finally called a halt as the sergeant entered.

'Well?' Chanworthy asked. 'Find anything?'

'Nothing at all, sir. No footprints around the windows. The flowerbeds are soft and too wide for anybody to jump across without leaving traces. The manservant says the front door was securely locked. We heard him draw the bolts back when we arrived, if you remember?'

'All right,' Chanworthy said, jerking his head. 'Get back downstairs, sergeant, and find out if the two domestics heard anything unusual and take this with you,' he added, gingerly passing over the decanter fragment. 'You'll find a cellophane wrapper in the car.' Then, turning to Helen, he announced, 'I'll take a look at Mr. and Mrs. Lonsdale.'

He raised Perry's right eyelid. After a moment or two he lowered it and did the same with Moira.

'Definitely drugged,' he said. 'Pinpoint pupils, slow pulse and breathing. Narcotic of some kind. However, they are in no danger. Do any of you know if either of them is addicted to sleeping tablets?'

The assembled quartet had no suggestions to offer. Chanworthy glanced about him and finally wandered into the adjoining dressing room. He returned a few minutes later.

'There's a phial of sleeping tablets in there,' he said.

He turned to the tray on which stood the coffee cups, percolator, cream and sugar. 'I'll get them analyzed,' he said.

'Does anybody know who ordered the coffee?'

'It was Mr. Lonsdale,' Helen said.

'He carried his wife up here after she

fainted; then a little later he came downstairs and told Pearson to have coffee prepared for his wife and himself. He — that is Mr. Lonsdale — took the tray himself. That's it on the table there.'

'Quite . . . Well, I'll have to talk it over with Mr. and Mrs. Lonsdale when they waken. I think I'd better get back downstairs. I'd like to see where the decanter was standing originally.'

All the presents were on the desk exactly as they had been in the morning — except for one decanter. The twin was still there with Helen's greeting card attached to it. Nearby lay the missing stopper.

'All very queer,' said the inspector thoughtfully, 'very queer indeed . . . '

'There is one thing which occurs to me,' Helen said slowly, 'the similarity between this attack and the bottle-top murder in Manchester. The circumstances are almost identical, only in this case it's a decanter whereas in the case of Joyce Kempton it was an eau-de-cologne bottle.'

'That had also occurred to me,' the

inspector said gravely, 'but there are times, Miss Ransome, when we get an imitative crime. Fortunately, as far as you were concerned, it did not develop into murder, but if it had have done there is the possibility your murderer might have been merely copying the Manchester killer. That does happen quite a lot, and it complicates the police work tremendously.'

'Sounds to me,' Dick Mills said, 'as though we're dealing with a homicidal maniac! Where's the point in it all, anyway? Why should anybody wish to murder Miss Ransome?'

'That's what I don't understand,' Helen put in. 'As far as I'm aware I have no enemies — or at least none vicious enough to wish to kill me.'

The inspector returned to another point. 'You said your wrist was seized when you tried to switch on the bed light, Miss Ransome. What sort of a grip was it?'

'It was an extremely strong one.'

'A man's — or a woman's?'

'That I can't say for sure.'

'And the room was totally dark?'

'Absolutely. The drapes were drawn.'

'In that case, Miss Ransome, somebody must have known the exact position of the bedside light. Your attacker could not have seen you reaching towards it but guessed that you would — and stopped you. That's very interesting . . . '

8

Both Perry and Moira were aware of something in the air long before they reached the breakfast table. They noticed it first in the queer way Pearson looked at them when he brought their tea. But the details came thick and fast when they entered the morning-room.

'And we slept through it all!' Moira exclaimed. 'I just can't believe it — though come to think of it I have got a bit of a headache.'

'I feel as if I had a hangover,' Perry growled. 'Drugged, you say? Both of us?'

'So it seems,' Betty Mills said. 'You were both asleep. The inspector took the coffee cups away for analysis, along with the percolator — as Helen's told you.'

'But there couldn't have been anything in the cups at least,' Perry protested. 'I fixed everything up with my own hands. Only Moira and I were anywhere near them once Pearson had brought the tray

78

into the drawing-room.'

'And Mrs. Carter prepared the coffee, sir,' Pearson put in gravely. 'I watched her do it.'

'Then it's beyond me,' Perry decided morosely. 'From the general outline, it sounds as though one of us here did it, and that's manifestly impossible. What's the inspector doing, did you say, Hel? Coming back this morning to question Moira and me?'

'So he said. Frankly, I got the idea that he didn't quite know what to make of things.'

'I'm not surprised,' Perry growled.

'At least we'll get the official facts when the police come,' Moira said. 'It all sounds dreadfully vague and impossible to me. Besides, who on earth would want to attack you, Hel?'

Helen laid her knife and fork gently down on her plate and looked at Moira.

'I believe I was nearly the second victim of the bottle-top murderer,' she stated.

'Doesn't sound very convincing to me,' Perry said, shaking his hand.

There was the faint clink of knives and

forks as Helen and Betty Mills went on with their breakfast. The others simply sat thinking. Pearson left the room as a sharp rap sounded at the front door.

'Chief Inspector Calthorp and Sergeant Dixon of the C.I.D. Scotland Yard, to see you, madam — sir,' he announced. 'Together with Inspector Chanworthy. I have shown them into the drawing-room.'

'Good morning, Mrs. Lonsdale — Mr. Lonsdale.' Calthorp held out his hand and his cadaverous face broke into a smile. 'This is Sergeant Dixon, and of course you know Inspector Chanworthy.'

'I do at least,' Perry replied. 'My wife doesn't.'

'Morning, Mrs. Lonsdale,' Chanworthy said gruffly.

'My reason for being here,' Calthorp explained, looking first at Perry and then Moira, 'is because there is definite reason for thinking the attack on Miss Ransome is connected with the slaying at Manchester.

'We have had the decanter top examined by the fingerprint experts, but there was nothing of interest. Neither

80

does poroscopy reveal anything — so in each case the attacker evidently took identical precautions.

'There are such things as imitative crimes, but I am satisfied the two attacks were made by the same person.

'Yes,' Perry admitted, frowning anxiously, 'it seems logical.'

'Naturally,' the chief inspector went on, 'we have not been idle since the murder of Joyce Kempton. As you may have seen in the newspapers, she had a young man friend by the name of Richard Lane, who disappeared after the girl's murder. We traced him as far as London. We have reason to believe he arrived two-and-a-half hours after the murder. A fast express could do it in that time, of course. After that the trail vanished.

'He had a second girl friend by the name of Sylvia Cotswood. We traced her through the ministry of labor. But when we went to her rooms, we learned she had departed about an hour before the death of Joyce Kempton, with all her belongings.

'We found out that Miss Cotswood had

taken the express for London — the same one, we believe, as Richard Lane.'

Perry moved impatiently in his chair. 'While admitting all this is very interesting, inspector, I still can't see what it has to do with the attack made on Miss Ransome.'

The inspector smiled gravely and looked at Moira.

'Don't you think it would be wiser to confess to the facts, Mrs. Lonsdale?' he asked. 'Evasion can't possibly serve any useful purpose now, you know.'

She was silent, her mouth a tight line. Perry started to rise, then sat down again.

'But look here, inspector — just a minute,' he protested. 'You can't be suggesting that my wife — '

'I'm not suggesting anything, Mr. Lonsdale; I'm stating a known fact — namely, that your wife, whatever her maiden name may have purported to be, is Sylvia Cotswood.'

'Since it's no use trying to hide it any longer, I may as well admit the truth,' Moira remarked quietly. 'I am Sylvia Cotswood. I knew I was making an incorrect statement on the marriage certificate, but a man in your position can take care of it if necessary, Perry.'

He stared at her blankly. 'But Moira, that isn't the point. You told me you'd come from Bristol and only arrived in London that very night — '

'I know I did,' Moira retorted. 'As a matter of fact, I had only just arrived in London, but it was from Manchester, not Bristol. My stenography job was in Manchester too, not Bristol. After all, you wouldn't expect me to link myself with a murder, would you?'

'Maybe I can help clear things up a little,' Calthorp said. Then, looking at Moira, he continued, 'Since you have been wise enough to admit your real identity, Mrs. Lonsdale, we can now tie up sundry points which so far have seemed unrelated. I believe that on your arrival in London you were involved — or at any rate, were a witness to — an attempted smash-and-grab raid on Millington's jewelry shop on North Brailsford Road?'

Moira looked at the thin, inscrutable

face in surprise, then nodded slowly.

'As a matter of fact, I was, but I'm puzzled as to how you know about it.'

'Call it co-operation between police departments,' Calthorp said. 'Divisional Inspector Latham, of the area where the incident occurred, had a few words with me concerning it, mainly because we have records at the Yard of the Farrish gang, and it looked like their work. It came out in conversation, and later was verified by statements you and Mr. Lonsdale signed, that you had been a witness to the affair. Your description tallied with that of Sylvia Cotswood. There was also a photograph — a snapshot the landlady's daughter took last summer — and you were in the group.'

'Oh!' Moira said, surprised. 'Yes, I remember it now.'

'You had my London address in full, inspector,' Perry snapped. 'Why didn't you get in touch with me? You must have known I would have some information about Moi — I mean Sylvia.'

'Oh yes, sir, we knew you probably would have,' Calthorp admitted. 'However, Mrs. Lonsdale, having run you to earth we were not particularly anxious to disturb you. In fact, we had no need to because we knew what you were doing — that you were intending to be wed to Mr. Lonsdale, that in fact you did marry him. Richard Lane is the one we want, and we felt sure that since he had trailed you to London, he would follow you here.'

'Now I begin to understand!' Perry exclaimed, his eyes brightening. 'You've been covering up for Lane, Moira! That's why you've been so evasive.'

'Yes,' she confessed. 'That's the truth, and there's no point in trying to conceal it . . . ' She looked at Calthorp. 'I'll give you the facts, inspector, just as they happened . . . On the night Joyce Kempton was murdered I had made up my mind to go and see her, chiefly to discover if we could come to some arrangement about Richard since Joyce and I were both deeply in love with him.

'I had just arrived outside her rooming-house when I saw Richard hurrying down the fire-escape. I ducked out of sight, but I could not help feeling he had seen me. I waited until he had gone, then entered by way of the front hall — in the ordinary way, of course.'

'Did anybody see you do so?' Calthorp demanded. 'The landlady, for instance?'

'Not as far as I'm aware. I went up to Joyce's room on the first floor and knocked on the door. When I couldn't get any answer, I sensed something was wrong, particularly as I recalled Dick's surprising behavior on the fire-escape.'

'Tell me, did you notice an aroma of eau-de-cologne?' Calthorp asked.

'Why — no.' Moira looked faintly surprised.

'I went round the building and up the fire-escape to the first floor, so I could see into the main living-room where Joyce lived. The room was in darkness, except for the reflection from an electric sign nearby. Joyce was lying sprawled on the floor — dead.'

Moira hesitated and pressed her hands to her eyes.

'By rights,' she continued, 'I should have gone to the police — but I love Dick, inspector, and I knew what it would mean for him if I did. So — I didn't.'

'I assume,' Calthorp said thoughtfully, 'That you had your suitcase with you, Mrs. Lonsdale?'

Moira nodded. 'That's right. When I left my rooms it was with the intention of leaving the district and trying my luck in London. Whatever arrangement I might have come to with Joyce concerning Dick, I knew in my heart that she had won him. That the best thing I could do was to cut him — and Joyce — right out of my life and leave the district.'

'I see. So you left after observing Joyce Kempton was dead — or apparently dead. What did you do then? Take the train for London?'

'Yes — and on the way, as I had to pass through a dark alley, Dick dived out of the shadows and tried to attack me. I managed to escape and got to the station. Whether or not Dick was following me I couldn't be sure, but I felt confident that once I reached London I would lose him completely . . .'

Sergeant Dixon sat behind the chief inspector, taking down her words in shorthand.

'When I reached London I just wandered out of the station,' Moira continued, 'wondering where I could put up for the night, when I got into the street where that smash-and-grab occurred — or nearly occurred. I encountered Mr. Lonsdale, we made our statements in the police station, and then when Mr. Lonsdale and I were having supper in a back street cafe, we saw Dick Lane peering through the window. There was murder in his face.'

'I can corroborate the cafe incident.' Perry said. 'I saw the man myself.'

'So far I have followed you perfectly,' the chief inspector said. 'What happened after that, Mrs. Lonsdale?'

She spread her hands helplessly.

'I admit quite frankly, inspector, that I was feeling pretty desperate. I needed protection. My one hope seemed to be to cling to Mr. Lonsdale. When he suggested an hotel for the night I was glad of it — '

'A quiet one — the Barryvale,' Perry put in. 'At first, inspector, I couldn't understand her dislike of busy places, company, and bright lights — but I can now. Obviously she was avoiding a chance meeting with Richard Lane.'

'Um,' Calthorp observed. 'So you stayed at the Barryvale, Mrs. Lonsdale. And a week later — yesterday to be exact — you were married.'

'Mr. Lonsdale wanted to marry me; he had this residence tucked away in the country, where I felt sure I could be safe. I jumped at the opportunity. But last night I saw Dick Lane again — '

9

Calthorp's cold eyes looked at her sharply. 'You did, eh? Where?'

'Outside the window of the drawing-room. He vanished almost immediately.'

'Yet, Mrs. Lonsdale, there are no footprints outside any of the windows,' Inspector Chanworthy interjected.

Calthorp nodded and asked, 'How close to the house was Lane, Mrs. Lonsdale?'

'Oh — maybe a couple of yards away. No more. Near enough for me to distinguish his features clearly.'

'Which means he must have been standing where the flower beds are,' Chanworthy remarked. 'I don't understand it.'

'I don't know anything about that,' Moira said anxiously, shaking her dark head. 'After all, the business of footprints and similar details are entirely police problems. All I know is that I saw Dick

Lane and that the discovery frightened me terribly for the moment. When I recovered from my faint, I found myself on the bed upstairs — and I stayed there, asking my husband to stay with me. To be candid, I was too scared to move.'

'And during the night,' Calthorp said slowly, staring hard at the carpet, 'Miss Ransome was attacked.'

'Yes, and I believe I know why.'

'You do?'

'I think it was a case of mistaken identity. Miss Ransome, as it happens, is very similar to me in appearance. Up until last night I had been using the room that Miss Ransome was occupying, whereas I had moved into next door with Mr. Lonsdale. I think Dick found out I had used that room and either was unaware of my marriage to Mr. Lonsdale, or had forgotten and assumed I would be there last night.'

The chief inspector arose and paced slowly up and down, still contemplating the carpet. At last he stopped and looked hard at Moira.

'I can see the possibilities of the

mistaken identity theory,' he said, 'but there are other points which I find it hard to reconcile. How did Richard Lane get hold of the decanter?'

'I think he must have entered the house after I had seen him, possibly by way of the fuel cellar. The door is not locked because Pearson uses it frequently. There is a concrete path, so there would be no footprints.'

'The fuel basement is a good idea,' Perry suggested. 'He could have got into the house that way, even though it doesn't explain how he looked through the window of the library without leaving prints in the flower bed.'

'As to that,' Calthorp said, 'it seems to me that if he could enter the house, he could also watch his chance to enter the library, from the inside, when nobody was watching . . . He could also have left the house by the same way he had entered — the fuel basement. That part is clear enough — but what about that coffee you and Mrs. Lonsdale drank?'

'I understand that it was drugged?' said Perry.

'It was. The analyst found traces of a sleeping remedy in the dregs of each cup, which tallied with the contents of a bottle in the medicine chest in your dressing room, Mr. Lonsdale. So, if Richard Lane made the mistake of attacking Miss Ransome instead of you, Mrs. Lonsdale, why did he go to the trouble of drugging the coffee? That fact alone shows that he must have known in which room you were sleeping.'

'All I can remember,' Perry said, frowning, 'is feeling very sleepy once I got to bed . . . '

'I have a suggestion to offer,' Moira said. 'Concerning the drugging, I mean. Pearson, besides being the manservant, is also the chauffeur and general factotum. He goes out to attend to the shopping and similar details. He hasn't been employed by my husband above six or seven weeks and — '

'Yes, that's true,' Perry broke in 'But I'm quite convinced that he's trustworthy.'

'Nobody is trustworthy if they're paid enough to be otherwise,' Moira said with conviction. 'At least, that has been my experience. For the sake of argument let's assume Dick Lane contacted Pearson and gave him a sedative.'

'Of the identical brand in the medicine chest?' Calthorp asked dubiously.

'Why not? That brand — it's my bottle, by the way — is known all over the country. Nothing unusual in that. Let's assume Dick gave Pearson these tablets, telling him to be sure that I got them in a drink on a certain night. He might not even have said they were sleeping tablets and have thrown Pearson off the scent that way ... Pearson had ample chance to put them in the cups, but not knowing which cup I'd use he put them in both. Dick, unaware of what happened — that I had married Mr. Lonsdale and changed rooms — believed I would be the only one to be drugged, and in that condition it would make killing me much easier.'

Calthorp gave a hard little smile.

'Well, thanks for the effort at a theory, Mrs. Lonsdale — but I'm afraid I'm unconvinced. Why didn't Pearson put the tablets in the percolator — and make sure? Why in the cups, where Mr. Lonsdale could have seen them?'

'Which I didn't,' Perry remarked.

'And the percolator has no sign of drug in it whatever,' Calthorp added. 'I'm afraid the right answer is greatly different to your hypothesis, Mrs. Lonsdale. However, I'll have a word with Pearson before I leave, though if he is involved in any such intrigue as you have suggested, obviously he won't admit it. Getting back to the main problem, Mrs. Lonsdale, why do you think Richard Lane tried to murder you?'

'Presumably because he knows I saw him leaving Joyce Kempton's rooming house.'

'True, but as you remarked yourself that does not imply that he killed her.'

'Within myself,' Moira said, 'I am perfectly sure he did kill her, even though tangible proof may be lacking at the moment. You see, I know him so well — and he is aware that as long as I am alive I might at any moment go to the police and tell everything. As far as I know, I'm the only witness who can prove he left the rooming-house about the time Joyce Kempton was murdered.'

'You say you know him so well — What can you tell me about him?'

'He's a man with a peculiar temperament.' Moira replied slowly. 'I used to put it down to plain impetuosity, but now all this has happened, I've altered my opinion. I think he's a maniac! And I'm not surprised he used glass. He hates it, inspector, in every shape and form. To him it's something brittle and deadly.'

'Which,' Calthorp remarked, 'carries us into the realm of psychiatry. And that is something about which I know less than nothing. Is that all you can tell me about him, Mrs. Lonsdale?'

'I'm afraid so,' Moira replied. 'I can only assume he murdered Joyce Kempton because his love had suddenly changed to hate. I've heard of such things but don't ask me the reason. As you say, that's a job for a psychiatrist.'

'Yes. Yes indeed.' The chief inspector pondered a moment or two, then he shrugged. 'Well, I think those are all the details I need for the moment, Mrs.

Lonsdale — Mr. Lonsdale, and thank you very much. I don't think we should have much difficulty in tracing Richard Lane now that you have seen him in this district.'

'The moment you do find him let me know right away,' Moira insisted. 'I shall never have a comfortable moment until I know he is under lock and key.'

'That I can quite understand,' Calthorp agreed.

'Moira,' said Perry, when the officers had gone, 'and I shall continue to call you that, by the way — why on earth didn't you tell me all this? I'd have understood.'

'You might not,' she answered, calmly. 'It needed something like that attack on Helen last night to bring things to a head. I'm happier than I can say that you have taken it the way you have.'

'But of course! As to the wrong statement on the marriage license, I'll soon straighten that out through my lawyers. What I do want you to know is that I'm full of admiration for the courageous way you've faced a particularly nasty situation. Knowing you are being chased by a killer is by no means pleasant.'

'It's ghastly,' Moira said with a little shiver. 'And the worst of it is, I'm still being chased — or at least I have that feeling, and it will remain until Calthorp sends word Richard has been caught.'

'Just the same, the situation has now changed completely.' Perry slipped his arm gently about Moira's shoulders. 'I know all the facts now and I'll be on the lookout. Lane won't be able to make one move without one of us knowing about it — even if we have to sleep in turns.'

Moira nodded moodily and remained silent for so long that Perry glanced at her in surprise.

'Don't let it worry you too much dearest,' he murmured. 'We can — '

'It wasn't that I was thinking about, Perry. I was just trying to imagine how the sleeping tablets got into our coffee. Do you suppose my guess about Pearson being mixed up in it is anywhere near the truth?'

'How can I say? Perhaps it is, since Calthorp didn't seem to follow up the idea with any particular enthusiasm. That's a police habit, to shut up the moment anything vital turns up. As you pointed out, Pearson's only been with me seven weeks, and even though his credentials did seem all right, he might be the type who's willing to accept a bribe.'

The problem hung with somber heaviness for a moment or two, then Perry took the girl's arm.

'Come on; we'll get back to the others and let them hear what we have been up to. They'll be anxious to know.'

'So here you are,' Will Ransome exclaimed eagerly. 'Well, what happened? The inspector dropped in here for a moment or two before leaving and asked us about our movements last night — then he left. What did he ask you?'

Perry hesitated and looked at Moira questioningly. She gave a slow nod.

'Sooner or later,' Perry said, 'the main facts are bound to leak out, and since they will sound all the more strange in official language, you might as well have the true version now, so ... ' And omitting nothing, he went into the complete details of the interview with Calthorp.

10

Beyond concurring here and there, Moira made no comment. Her dark blue eyes moved from face to face and she beheld varying expressions from sheer amazement to horror. When the story was finished Will Ransome gave a low whistle.

'Well, the effect it has on me is to make me feel several kinds of a heel,' he exclaimed. 'I'm afraid, Moira, that I had you down as a moody and even mentally lazy sort of person and of no possible use as a wife for Perry. Now I realize how completely I misjudged you. No wonder you were moody with all that on your mind!'

'Thanks, Will.' Moira flashed him a grateful smile.

'I think all of us felt pretty much the same as Will,' Betty Mills commented. 'Especially Helen. So we are tendering a sincere apology — if you'll accept it?'

'Accept it? Of course I will, Betty, I

quite understand how things must have looked.'

Helen, who had been standing pondering with a finger pressed against her cheek, suddenly seemed to reach a decision.

'Look, Moira, you and Perry were going to honeymoon in the south of France. Why on earth didn't you? It's most unlikely that Richard Lane would ever have been able to follow you that far. You'd have been perfectly safe. Why did you insist on staying here?'

'I just didn't feel up to it — and I still don't.'

'Oh . . . ' Helen nodded, even though she did not appear convinced. 'I see — Well, I think you should know what my reaction is to this whole horrible business. I have decided to leave.'

'Leave?' Moira repeated. 'But for why?'

'Why? I get half-murdered and you ask me why! Because I'm scared of the same thing happening again, since it is a possibility as long as Richard Lane remains free, and I don't propose to take the chance. I'm going home where I can feel safe — more or less.'

'It's up to you, of course,' Perry admitted. 'We'd have been more than glad if you'd have stayed on for a day or two.'

'Not for me, Perry, thanks!' Helen patted his arm and gave him a warm smile. 'I used to like this rambling old pile, but times change — as the saying is. I'm pretty sure Moira and you will be happier without me. I've monopolized a good deal, I'm afraid, and all I can say is I'm sorry. I think I'll go and pack.'

'I'm afraid,' Will Ransome said, 'that with Helen the mainspring gone it doesn't leave much for the other little cogs.' He grinned fatuously. 'I may as well go back with her. What about you two?' he added, glancing at Betty and her husband.

'Well, it's probably about time for us to see how the business is getting on,' Dick Mills said. 'Can't afford to be away too long, you know, bad for the bank account.'

'Besides,' Betty put in, 'we just don't belong in the house of a honeymoon couple. I thought it was wrong right from the start, and now after what has happened, I'm sure of it . . . I think we should go.'

The three left the room and Moira gave a tired, half-smile as she glanced at Perry.

'Like rats on a sinking ship,' she remarked.

'Oh, I wouldn't say that, dearest. They're just — jittery, and I don't blame them. Ask yourself: would you stay in a house where murder was nearly committed?'

Moira did not answer. There was a faraway look in her eyes that Perry could not fathom.

After the guests had gone, an air of gloom seemed to descend on the manor. Perry found himself wondering what had really happened as he sat in a deep easy chair considering Moira on the opposite side of the blazing fire. He wondered if the four had gone out of sheer respect for the honeymoon couple, or whether — odious thought — they had gone to show their contempt for the machinations of Sylvia Cotswood.

This latter possibility Perry refused to admit. He still loved Moira — and there was an end of it. But just the same — he looked at the girl again. She was half-crouched on a huge leather buffet, just within range of the tall reading lamp. Apparently quite lost to her surroundings, she was reading steadily. The drapes were drawn. The air smelled warm. The silence was intense.

'Just as though we'd been married for years and getting in our dotage,' Perry observed bitterly.

Moira kept on reading. Perry gave her an impatient look.

'For goodness sake, Moira, what is that you're so engrossed in? You've had your nose buried in it ever since dinner.'

She started and glanced up. 'This? Oh — I'm sorry, Perry. I didn't realize . . . ' She laid the book on the rug beside her. 'It's Adams' *Atavism of the Mind*.'

'It's — what?' Perry gave a blank stare for a moment; then he remembered something. 'Oh yes, I know. One of those books you carried around in your suitcase. I've seen 'em now you come to mention it. But what on earth do you find in any of them that's so interesting?'

'I am wondering,' she answered, gazing absently into the fire, 'what makes Dick Lane's mind tick.'

'So you're still thinking about him, are you?' Perry leaned forward in his chair, elbows on his upthrust knees, his profile etched by the firelight. 'Moira dear, I do wish you wouldn't! It can't do any good to keep remembering him.'

'But I knew him so well,' she answered, glancing. 'I've been trying to find out for quite a time now what turns a decent person — for in the main he is decent — into a maniacal killer. It can only be something in the mind, can't it?'

'Presumably — but I'd rather leave that sort of stuff to the psychiatrists. It's hardly our meat.'

'I'm the sort of person who likes to find out things for myself,' Moira said. 'The moment I suspected something was queer with Dick I bought several of these books and studied them. Over and over again I've read them, but I can't seem to find the answer. I can only think that he's a victim of hereditary influence, that he suffered a shock at an early age — or something like that. One thing I have found, though, is the correct name for his intense dislike of glass. It's crystalophobia, which means an insane dread of glass objects, or sometimes it's called hyalophobia, which means fear of glass.'

'Well now you do know, how much good does it do you?' Perry asked.

'None, since you put it that way, but I am interested. From your tone I gather that you are not.'

'All I'm interested in is the fact that you are my wife and that we were married yesterday — that so far we've had nothing but worry and trouble and that sitting here, we look like a couple of old fogies who have about 20 grandchildren scattered over the earth. It's crazy! It's unnatural! I think the police should be trusted to look after Richard Lane and we should go to the south of France as we planned. Otherwise this place is liable to kill us through sheer boredom.'

Perry leaned forward, picked up the

book, closed it and set it down emphatically on the table at his side.

'On Monday,' he decided, 'we're going up to London for the day. We'll drive over — just ourselves without Pearson. We'll have dinner, see a show, then spend the night at the flat and return next day. That'll just be the beginning of the toning-up process.'

'Toning-up process?' Moira looked puzzled.

'Your nerves want bucking up, dearest, and the surest way to do that is to get into brightness and company, see things, forget all about the beastliness which has been surrounding you.'

Moira pondered long and earnestly, then she smiled.

'All right, Perry, if you say so. Maybe it will do me good at that . . . '

★   ★   ★

The Metz, Perry's favorite restaurant, was located below the level of the London main street and to reach it Perry and Moira had to pass down a narrow, dark alley and then descend a flight of steps.

Perry felt Moira draw back with instinctive dread as they went into the abyss, but he held her arm tightly and murmured words of encouragement. Then the brightly lighted glass tops of the swing doors of the Metz appeared and in another moment or two they were in the vast dining room.

A waiter came forward to greet them. 'Mr. Lonsdale! Well, I am glad to see you again, sir! It must be five or six years since you were in.'

'Quite that, Peter,' Perry smiled. 'Thanks for the welcome. You don't get any fatter, I notice.'

The waiter paused and eyed Moira in polite respect.

'Mrs. Lonsdale,' Perry explained — and Moira turned.

The waiter bowed gravely. 'So — good evening, madam. May I express my congratulations — Now let me see, I think I can find a table in the position you used to like, Mr. Lonsdale. We get very crowded these days, unfortunately — that is, for the diners. Hardly for trade.'

'Menus have changed and food with them.' Perry sighed, studying the white oblong of card. 'As far as I'm concerned I'll take the best you can offer and rely on your judgment — Have you any particular wish, dear?'

Moira shook her head.

'No, I don't think so.' She smiled at the waiter. 'If my husband can trust your judgment, I'm sure I can.'

'Thank you, madam ... And — er — champagne, sir? In the usual way?'

'Yes, I — '

'But not for me,' Moira said with quiet firmness. 'Call me old-fashioned if you like, but I prefer coffee.'

'Then I'll do likewise,' Perry sighed. 'She's going to make a temperance reformer out of me before she's finished, Peter!'

The waiter smiled and moved away. Perry glanced about him genially and rubbed his palms softly together.

'Well?' he asked. 'Much better than sitting at home rotting in the drawing-room, isn't it?'

'You're just dying for me to say that it

is aren't you?' she chided. 'I'm sorry, Perry, but nice though it is — and much though I appreciate all you've done — I still prefer the quiet of the country. I can't help the way I'm made, can I?'

'Well no, but — ' Perry hesitated. 'Isn't it rather a selfish viewpoint?'

'But Perry, this sounds so unlike you! Actually you make it appear as though you're angry.'

'No.' He shook his head and smiled tautly. 'Not exactly angry, Moira; it's just that I don't want you to start developing into a — '

Perry stopped, glancing up in surprise as he found Peter beside him again.

Just behind the waiter stood a bulky, good-natured looking man of middle age in a dress suit.

'Begging your pardon, Mr. Lonsdale . . . ' Peter's voice came in a respectful murmur. 'Shortage of floor space these days. More diners than we can cater for . . . Would you mind very much if this gentleman were to share your table? This is a table for four, after all.'

'Why not at all — Do we, Moira?'

The girl shrugged and made no response, Peter breathed a little harder and gave a slight nod; then the newcomer loomed into the picture as Perry got to his feet.

The man was probably a good 200 pounds and close on six feet tall. He breathed asthmatically as he levered himself down at the table.

'Done it,' he observed, with a wry smile. 'You do forgive my barging in like this, I hope?'

'Of course,' Perry assured him, settling down again. 'Don't mention it. May I introduce ourselves? This is my wife, Mrs. Lonsdale. I'm Perry Lonsdale.'

11

The man considered him after he had glanced at Moira.

'Perry Lonsdale, eh? Let me see now — I've heard of you somewhere. The name, at least . . . '

'You're probably thinking of the Lonsdale Shipping Line. My father owned it; now I do likewise. Or perhaps you saw my name in the social columns. I find it mighty difficult to keep out of them.'

'Well now . . . I'm Adam Castle — Dr. Adam Castle. I'm what is commonly called a neurologist, or nerve specialist. I have my rooms over in Harley Street.'

'I imagine the post-war cases keep you pretty busy,' Perry commented.

'Oh yes, business is brisk enough. You live in London, of course?'

'Well, partly.' Perry said. 'My wife and I are staying at our country home — the Larches in Somerset. Near Brinhampton.'

'I don't know Brinhampton, but I do

know Somerset.' Adam Castle wagged his head approvingly. 'Beautiful country. Used to go there a lot as a young man.'

Perry and Moira sipped their soup and the neurologist's blue eyes surveyed the restaurant with an air of good humored tolerance.

'Prefer London to Somerset?' he inquired finally.

'I do — my wife doesn't. Actually we're domiciled in Somerset. Only up here for a change. Going back tomorrow.'

'Um . . . You know,' Castle went on. 'I have the feeling that my presence at this table is a decided intrusion. You were talking quite freely when I came along, but since then you've hardly said a word to each other. I wish you would. I don't like to feel I've spoiled your fun.'

'But you haven't,' Perry said. 'Besides, I've been talk — ' He stopped and smiled wryly. 'Oh, you mean my wife hasn't spoken much? That's simply because she isn't the talkative type.'

'I don't blame you, Mrs. Lonsdale.' Castle looked at her. 'If it comes to that, there isn't much to talk about these days,

113

is there? Unless it be austerity or crime, neither of which appeals to me.'

'Crime?' Perry repeated. 'Oh — yes. There seem to be plenty of murders from children to . . . salesgirls.'

'Uh-huh. A natural reaction after the war, you know. At least, I think so. Minds are not yet back to normal after the horrors of guns, bombs, black-outs and air raids. Delicate thing, the mind.'

'You mean.' Moira said, 'that neurology covers the science of the brain as well?'

Castle regarded her for a few moments.

'Well, no,' he said finally. 'I wouldn't say that. A neurologist is only interested in the brain as a nervous organ — as the seat of all nervous reaction, in fact. The science of the brain is really the science of the mind — in the medical world, anyway, and it takes a psychiatrist to deal with that.'

'A distinction with a difference,' Perry observed.

'Exactly so. And though I am a neurologist, I believe that all things originate in the mind and leave their mark on the body. But let me add,' — Castle

114

raised a pink finger — 'that that is only my personal opinion. If I were to mention it before the medical faculty I'd probably get thrown out on my ear,' he chuckled.

Moira seemed to be pondering over a question, and Perry fancied he knew what it was. He remembered the books on mental quirks that she had been reading. It was possible that the idea of mentioning the various theories she had absorbed had occurred to her but she changed her mind and remained silent.

'If there's one place you should steer away from tonight, it's the Arts Hall in Holborn,' Castle said presently. 'Avoid it like a plague.'

'Why?' Moira asked in surprise.

'Because I'm giving a lecture there,' Castle laughed.

'Will that be so very terrible?' Perry asked.

'It would to young people like you. It's open to the public, of course, but you've got to be medically-minded to enjoy the stuff. I don't relish it myself but I have to do it because it's my profession, my father was determined I should be a neurologist, or else!' The silvery head shook firmly. 'No, nothing in it for you two. What do you care about the parietal lobe, the fissure of sylvius, the cortex cerebri, and so forth? In a word, my friends I am giving a lecture on the brain and its nervous relationship to physical behavior.'

'Which sounds as though it should be very interesting,' Moira commented.

'My dear Mrs. Lonsdale, you're joking,' Castle protested.

'No, really: I'm quite intrigued.'

Castle glanced at each in turn. Then he turned to Moira.

'Tell me Mrs. Lonsdale, why are you so interested? Have you been a medical student at some time, are you writing a medical treatise, or what is the reason?'

'Well, I — It's a personal matter, really.' Moira gave him a frank look. 'I happen to know somebody who behaves in a queer way and I think the cause is mental. I've spent a lot of time trying to dig the facts out of textbooks, but of course they can't compare with a lecture.'

'If there's any way in which I can help

you . . . What seems to be wrong with this friend of yours?'

'I — I'd rather not say. It's personal.'

'Then of course you can't expect much aid from me, can you?' The neurologist resumed his meal. 'I can hardly be expected to guess at what you want to know.'

Moira smiled. 'I don't want you to do anything, Dr. Castle. Just listening to you will be enough for me; I'll pick up all the information I need.'

'Oh, this is absurd,' Perry protested. 'Listen doctor, there just isn't any point in my wife behaving in this fashion. She's taking on to her own shoulders a responsibility for which there isn't the slightest necessity.'

'That's a matter of opinion,' Moira said curtly.

Adam Castle raised and lowered his massive shoulders. 'I'm not going to say anything one way or the other,' he said. 'I make it a rule never to interfere in the arguments of other people; it's safer in the long run. My wife and I have lived harmoniously for the past 20 years by never arguing about anything . . . ' He considered them blandly. 'Make your own choice my friends, but I'll wager you'd find the theater much more entertaining.'

Perry gave Moira a grim glance. He could see her hesitating as she tried to make up her mind. Then, glancing at his watch, the big neurologist got up from the table. Moira looked up at him quickly.

'Where did you say this lecture is to be doctor? The Arts Hall?'

'Yes — in Holborn. Not 10 minutes away.' Castle glanced at Moira curiously, then signaled the waiter. 'It starts at 7.30 if you're interested.'

'I shall be there,' Moira decided. 'Even if my husband is not.'

'Up to you.' Castle pulled out his wallet and produced two visiting cards.

'Here — these will give you good seats — if you wish to come.'

'Have you gone completely crazy?' Perry asked heatedly after the doctor had gone.

'Of course not. I simply want to help Dick Lane, gather all the facts I can for when he comes to trial.' Moira replied curtly.

'You want to help a murderer? It isn't even reasonable, Moira, and you know it!'

'It isn't reasonable to you, perhaps, because you've never met Dick and haven't the least idea how he behaves when he's normal. As I've told you, I believe he does the things he does because of some mental kink. Once he is captured and bundled before judge and jury he won't have a chance. They'll condemn and hang him on the evidence. I want to prevent that. I'd like to prove,' Moira finished absently, 'that he is sick mentally. That is to say, he can no more help committing a crime than he can help having a toothache. You don't think of sending a man to jail for having a toothache, do you?'

'There's no comparison Moira. But what do you suppose you can do about it? You're just an ordinary person with no qualifications. You don't think the law would take any notice of you, do you?'

'But they would pay attention to a man like Dr. Castle. If I can only get to know him well enough I'd like him to put in a word or two on Dick's behalf.'

'I doubt if his opinion would be admissible,' Perry said. 'He's a neurologist, not a psychiatrist. There's a world of difference.'

'Please, Perry, try and see it my way Moira urged. 'You wouldn't want to see an innocent man hanged, would you?'

'Innocent? After what he did to Joyce Kempton and tried to do to Helen Ransome?'

'I put it badly, she said. 'I mean an — er — irresponsible man. I'm quite sure he did those things because of some sort of mental black-out.'

Perry raised his hands, then dropped them helplessly.

'All right, you win — as usual. At least I don't want it thrown at me in the future that I let a man die because of my selfishness. We'll go — and I'll bet we're bored to tears!'

The lecture hall was warm and Perry dozed spasmodically. But not Moira. She sat stiffly erect, hand clenched on top of her handbag listening intently to the ponderous speaker.

'It's over my head.' Perry grumbled half aloud during one of his wakeful moments.

'Not very flattering to Dr. Castle, I must say,' Moira said bitterly. 'He looked at you once or twice, and I'm not surprised.'

Perry smothered a yawn and got to his feet. Castle had finally stopped talking. There was a stir in the hall as some folk departed and others clustered in little groups to discuss the profundities of the brain.

As he helped Moira on with her fur cape, Perry was approached by a tightlipped man of about 40 who had sat next to him.

'Clever man Castle,' he said. 'Do you know I never thought there could be such complexity attaching to the fissure of Rolando.'

'Neither did I,' Perry muttered.

'Just goes to show what a wide range of knowledge these psychiatrists have. I should think Dr. Castle is one of the best in the city today — bar none. Well,' — the man nodded briefly — 'good night.'

Perry frowned and hesitated, glancing at Moira who was also looking surprised. Then Perry turned away swiftly.

'I say just a moment — !'

The man paused. Yes?'

'Did you say psychiatrist?' Perry asked.

'Why, yes.' The man looked surprised.

'But I understood he was a neurologist.'

'He is — but he's also a psychiatrist. One of the cleverest in London . . . Do excuse me will you? There's a chap over there I must speak to.'

12

'Well, well, so here you are?' Adam Castle came toward them. He was beaming with good humor. 'How did it go down? I noticed that it lulled you to sleep, Mr. Lonsdale — and at that I'm not in the least surprised. It's a subject that is as dry as dust when you're not really interested . . . But you, Mrs. Lonsdale, never took your eyes from me the whole time. I feel most complimented!'

'I found it most fascinating,' she said.

'That's good. We — '

'I'd like to ask you a question, doctor,' Perry interrupted, his voice unusually sharp. 'I've just heard from a member of the audience that you are a psychiatrist — one of the greatest in London.'

Castle chuckled.

'So you found out, did you? I expected you would, sooner or later. But I'm hardly the greatest in London. There's a chap called Dexter who's forgotten all I ever learned . . . Oh, I see your point. You're wondering why I didn't mention it in the first place?'

'I am,' Perry assented flatly.

'Well, Mr. Lonsdale, it's quite simple. Tell the average person that you are a psychiatrist and he's scared stiff. Most people expect a psychiatrist to start probing with a hypnotic eye and delving into their mind.'

'What you mean is, you thought we'd be scared,' Perry suggested. 'That it?'

'Not exactly scared, but I did think it would put you both off your stroke. I like people to be happy and at ease and unfortunately my profession is a strong deterrent to that. Under the circumstances I'm sure you will forgive the little deception.'

'Of course,' said Moira. 'And I thought your lecture was wonderful doctor.'

'Good!' He beamed upon her. 'Did it answer any of your own particular problems?'

'Well — no, I wouldn't say that it did. You barely touched on the topics which really interest me.'

'That was my last lecture for the present,' he said. 'I am taking a fortnight's vacation before the summer. A motor trip with my wife, as usual, I expect. Anyway, perhaps I may see you again.'

'Never can tell,' Moira replied.

'Rather a wonderful man, don't you think so?' she asked Perry as they left the building.

'Genial enough, anyway,' Perry responded. 'I can't help feeling, though, that I've been compelled to waste a perfectly good evening. Nor can I see what particular benefit it has been to you. No use trying to enlist his aid on behalf of Lane for the next couple of weeks, anyway.'

'Yes,' Moira admitted moodily. 'Which is a pity. But even if Dick is caught, he won't be brought to trial until the summer assizes and that's a good way off yet. In the meantime I'll try and think of the best way to approach Castle. I'm sure he would be able to help.'

Perry hailed a newspaper boy who was vociferously advertising his wares at the curb edge. Stuffing the paper in his coat pocket, he took Moira's arm and guided her along the street to the garage where they had left the car.

They had hardly got into the flat and put the lights on before Moira said anxiously: 'You did get a paper, didn't you, Perry? Yes, there it is in your pocket.'

He handed it to her and she commenced reading without even bothering to remove her hat or cape.

'Your beloved friend, Richard Lane, still on your mind, eh?' Perry asked dryly.

'Of course he is. I want to see if the police have found him yet.'

'Then I'll go and make some coffee and sandwiches — if you can stick canned stuff. That's about all we have here.'

Moira said nothing, just went on reading.

'They haven't got him yet,' Moira announced, when he returned from the kitchen. 'Nor is there any mention of the information we gave Inspector Calthorp on Saturday morning.'

'Hardly likely there would be,' Perry said as he poured the coffee. 'The police don't hand out information of that sort to the press: it's confidential. What does the report say exactly?'

Moira looked down at the newspaper again.

'The police investigation into the brutal murder of Joyce Kempton, the Manchester salesgirl, who was found dead in her room, March 9, was carried a stage further recently when Chief Inspector Calthorp of Scotland Yard visited the Somerset area. Chief Inspector Calthorp told the press he was satisfied with progress to date, but asked that anybody who might have information regarding Richard Lane, Viaduct Street, Manchester, would notify the police immediately. So far, Lane has evaded the nationwide search, but Scotland Yard has reason to believe there will be important developments in the near future.'

'Which doesn't tell very much,' Perry observed, holding out the plate of sandwiches. 'Wonder where he's hiding out? You'd think hunger would have driven him into the open by now.'

'Yes, you would.' Moira lowered the paper and nibbled the sandwich absently.

'And as long as he remains free, I'm afraid for myself.'

'Why?' Perry asked. 'If, as seems possible, he killed Joyce Kempton during a mental blackout — and tried to attack Helen while in a similar condition — they represent only occasional instances. He must be normal between times. And during his — er — calm moments, you have nothing to fear from him, have you?'

'No, probably not — but how am I to know when he's normal? You must remember that he hates me because he knows I saw him leave the scene of the crime.'

It was just after 9 o'clock the following morning when they set out for Somerset. The air was warm, there was scarcely any breeze, and the city sparkled in the early sunshine.

When they reached Westbury, they stopped for lunch, then continued on. It was close to 4 o'clock when they drove into Somerset. Only 20 miles to Brinhampton. The road was fairly quiet; the heavy holiday traffic would not commence for at least another month.

'That looks like trouble ahead,' Perry remarked suddenly and Moira, who had been lying back sunning herself, straightened up and peered ahead through the windshield.

A car was drawn up at the side of the road and a man was bending over the engine. As Perry drew alongside, he glanced up. The bright afternoon sunshine glinted on the silvery waves in his hair. He had an enormous body, was tremendously stout.

'For the love of Mike, it's Dr. Castle!' Perry gasped in astonishment.

'How on earth did he get here?'

Moira frowned slightly.

'Well, he did say something about a motor tour. Just the same, it's a remarkable coincidence.'

'I say, old man I wonder if you'd — Great Scott! Mr. and Mrs. Lonsdale!' Castle broke off blankly. 'Well, by all that's remarkable! How are you? Say, don't mind me not shaking hands will you? I'm covered with oil — my dear!' he called to his wife, who was watching the proceedings from the front seat of the big

Daimler, 'it's Mr. and Mrs. Lonsdale.'

Perry climbed out of his car.

'What seems to be the trouble, doctor? Engine break down?'

'Apparently. My abilities are confined to repairing the ills of human beings, not the breakdowns of mechanically propelled vehicles. If I'd had the chauffeur with me he'd have fixed it in no time. But I gave him a fortnight's holiday. Like to see what you can do?'

Perry inspected the big car. His own mechanical ability was by no means great, and an engine of this size and make had him completely baffled.

'Afraid I can't help you doctor. Far as I can tell, everything seems to be in order.'

'That's just the trouble,' Castle sighed. 'A car always does appear to be in order when it goes wrong. We were sailing along merrily, and suddenly it stopped. And I can't make it budge.'

'Since it cut out abruptly, it likely is the ignition, doctor,' Perry opined. 'Afraid it's a job for an expert. You have plenty of petrol?'

'Sure I have,' Castle acknowledged.

'Seems to be nothing else for it but to wait until an R.A.C. patrol comes along. If you pass one, you might tip him off for me — or else tell the first garage you come to. I want to be moving. Haven't had lunch yet and the wife's feeling tired. Likes her cup of tea, you know — and so do I.'

'That settles it then,' Moira said. 'Come along with us and have lunch at the Larches. We're only about 15 miles away. We can stop at a garage on the way and tell them to pick up your car.'

'Well . . . ' The psychiatrist shrugged and put on his jacket. 'It's confoundedly decent of you. Come along, my dear.'

In a few minutes the changeover was complete even to luggage. The psychiatrist and his wife settled in the back seat and Perry climbed in behind the wheel. Two miles farther down the road they stopped at a garage and Castle gave his instructions to the mechanic.

'Right, sir, we'll bring it in right away,' the man said. 'Where can I get in touch with you?'

'Er — that's a point.' Castle frowned. 'I — '

'The Larches, Brinhampton,' Perry said quickly. 'It's the Lonsdale residence. Ring up there.'

'That I will, sir.'

'And do the job as quickly as you can,' Castle added, settling back in the soft upholstery. 'You've no idea how much my wife and I appreciate this.'

'We do indeed,' Mrs. Castle agreed.

'Quite all right,' Perry smiled. 'There's more room at the Larches than we can ever use, so consider yourselves our guests for as long as you wish.'

'Give, and it shall be given unto you,' Castle said cheerfully, spreading his hands. 'I'm always telling my wife that. It gets you out of a hole at a critical moment.'

Pearson opened the big oak door and came down the steps.

'Good afternoon, madam — sir,' he greeted. 'Welcome back.'

His eyes strayed to Castle and his wife.

'You'll find the bags in the rear, Pearson,' Perry said. 'Ours and — Oh, this is Dr. Adam and Mrs. Castle, friends of ours. They'll be staying indefinitely. You might tell Mrs. Carter to make the necessary arrangements.'

'Very good, sir.' Pearson stared at the genial, double-chinned face of the psychiatrist for a moment, then turned to the car and the luggage.

'My word,' Adam Castle kept reiterating, as he waddled into the great hall and looked about him. 'If it doesn't sound too unmannerly, Lonsdale, I'm thinking it's a good job we did break down. Worth it to come here. Magnificent place you've got! Magnificent!'

13

Adam Castle settled down in an easy chair and puffed gently.

'Splendid!' he declared, craning his flabby neck as he took in the details of the room. 'So tastefully arranged — I think I detect a woman's hand here.'

Perry grinned.

'Well yes, you do — but not my wife's. The arrangement of this room was done by a Miss Ransome, a close lady friend of mine. My wife and I were only married last Saturday,' he added quickly, realizing that his statement probably sounded strange.

'You're newlyweds!' Castle ejaculated; then he glanced at his wife. 'And last night you were saddled with an old walrus like me when you were trying to enjoy yourselves! And now I'm actually in your home! Oh no, this won't do at all. The moment the car's fixed, we're off. Why, you're on your honeymoon!'

'Sort of,' Perry grudgingly admitted.

'Sort of?' he repeated. 'It's the accepted thing, isn't it?'

'Yes, of course it is, only — '

Moira broke in: 'We're taking a proper honeymoon later on, Dr. Castle. In the south of France. At the moment, circumstances won't permit it.'

'Oh, well then, that's different.' Adam Castle looked benevolent again. 'I'd never have forgiven myself if we had barged in on a honeymoon couple — Ah!' His blue eyes gleamed as Pearson entered with tea. 'This looks more like it!'

Perry dismissed Pearson with a nod and Moira settled down to the task of pouring tea while Perry served the sandwiches.

'Well, we're sort of marooned.' Castle gave a bronchial chuckle. 'Can't think of a better place to be marooned, either. Since you insist, we accept your hospitality, of course, but only on one condition.'

'Condition?' Perry waited, surprised.

'That I receive a violent jab in the ribs if I even mention psychiatry. This is a vacation for me — and I know for a fact,

Lonsdale, that you are not interested in the science.'

'But I am,' Moira asserted. 'Most interested.'

'Alas yes, I'm aware of that, but let's leave it alone until I return to normal working hours, shall we?'

'Yes of course, if you wish,' Moira said in a faintly disappointed tone.

There was a gentle tap on the door and Pearson entered silently.

'I have made the necessary arrangements with the housekeeper, sir,' he announced. 'The mauve room has been prepared for Dr. and Mrs. Castle and the luggage taken there. And Meadow View Garage is on the line asking for Dr. Castle.'

'Oh, that'll be about the car.' Castle heaved ineffectually and flopped back into the easy chair. 'My word, I get heavier!' he complained. 'I say, Lonsdale, would you mind seeing what they have to say?'

'Pleasure,' Perry assured him, and left the room. He was back in a few moments and met Adam Castle's expectant blue eyes.

'Fixed?' he asked quickly.

'Afraid not, doctor, in fact it looks as though you and Mrs. Castle will be with us for a day or two at least. Short-circuit somewhere. Under present conditions, it will take three or four days to locate the trouble and make the necessary repairs.'

Adam Castle finished the third sandwich, cast a longing glance at a fourth and then steeled himself. He heaved to his feet with the grace of a hippopotamus leaving a pond.

'I'm certainly going to like it here,' he decided looking about him again. 'My word I am!'

By the time dinner had come and gone, the obese psychiatrist seemed thoroughly at home. So much so that he looked more like the host than the guest as the four of them sat in the drawing-room.

'Since your trip has been spoiled, doctor,' Perry said, 'we might take one in my car, starting tomorrow. We can use the house as our base, and take a different journey each day until your car is ready. At least it will be a change. There's nothing worse than four walls to cramp the mind.'

'There,' Adam Castle said calmly, 'you reveal true psychology. If more people realized that it is the limitations of their surroundings which mold their minds, we would be a better race. Believe it or not, the breeding grounds of disease and crime are — '

'Adam!' his wife cautioned gently.

'Eh? Yes, my dear?' He glanced at her and then grinned. 'Oh, sorry! I'd forgotten that I wasn't going to talk shop . . . Yes indeed, a grand idea.'

Castle's eyes strayed to the table beside Moira's chair.

'What do I see there?' he asked at length. 'Are they books on the mind?'

Moira nodded. She had put all six books there earlier in the evening for just such a moment as this.

Adam Castle held out his chubby hand and one by one Moira handed the books to him. She glanced at Perry but his face was expressionless.

'The only one that is any good is Ferri's *Criminal Sociology*, Castle pronounced at length, dumping the other five books on the carpet beside his chair. 'I think his chapter on 'The Data of Criminal Anthropology, in which he shows the psychological differences between the habitual and occasional criminal, is about one of the best treatises on the subject I've ever read.' The pink hands flipped through the pages. 'Yes indeed! I observe that you, too, have given this chapter particular attention, Mrs. Lonsdale.'

'I most certainly have,' Moira assented. 'I was particularly interested in the case of Moral, concerning the impulse to crime. You will remember — I think it's page 43 — that he mentions how one day when he was crossing a bridge in Paris he saw a man gazing into the water. The homicidal idea of throwing the man into the water occurred to him, so strongly indeed that he had to flee from the temptation.

'There is also the case of Humboldt's nurse who was assailed one day by the temptation to kill her charge — and resisted it. Then there's the instance of Brierre de Boismont who tells of a learned intellectual who, at the sight of a picture in the public art gallery, was overwhelmed by the desire to cut it out of its frame. All instances of people consumed by a brief, devouring impulse which in each case was mastered.'

There was a thoughtful expression in the psychiatrist's eyes. The book was lying on his knees, but he was not reading it. He was looking intently at Moira.

'I recall the instances perfectly,' he said presently. 'And what they do is simply represent what happens to all of us in a great or small way. There is not a person living who has not at one time or another felt an irresistible urge to be animalistic, sadistic, even obscene, and yet in nine cases out of 10 the impulse is quenched by decency and innate uprightness of character.'

'There are those,' Moira said, 'who cannot quench it. For them I cannot feel anything but pity.'

'For a young woman, newly married, your interest in criminal psychology is little short of incredible,' he commented. 'And here am I back on my old topic just after vowing I wouldn't talk about it while on my vacation.'

'But surely there's no harm in intelligent conversation?' Moira asked. 'You are here with us — you are a famous psychiatrist — and there is such a lot I'd like to verify. Whom better to ask than you?'

'I appreciate the flattery,' Castle smiled. 'All right then, what is it you wish to know?'

'Just this — and please don't think it too strange. Do you believe that a criminal, a homicidal murderer, really is a fiend, or is he a very sick man?'

Castle blinked and took his pipe out of his mouth.

'My word, what a question! In one breath you pose a problem which the law, science, and psychiatry has batted about like a shuttlecock for the last 10 years and more. There are three separate answers, Mrs. Lonsdale. In the eyes of the law the homicidal maniac is an outcast of society and must be sentenced to death; in the eyes of science, he is atavistic, a throwback to some recessive unit in his parental strain where a like tendency to crime was exhibited; in the eyes of psychiatry, he is a man whose mind is ill — '

'That's it!' Moira's eyes gleamed as she interrupted. 'Ill mentally. Therefore, he could be cured.'

'That,' Adam Castle said, 'is debatable. It would depend upon the tenacity of the warp gripping his mind. He might be tractable, he might not. It is by no means easy to turn a criminal mind into a normal one. The damage already has been done. It is like trying to repair a broken machine that from the start has had friction in the wrong places. Usually the criminal mind is a criminal mind because of childhood environment. As the twig is bent . . . '

Adam Castle sucked thoughtfully on his pipe. Perry shifted a trifle uncomfortably. The least perturbed of all was Mrs. Castle. She sat calmly in the basket chair near her husband, waiting for the conversation to resume.

'I suppose,' Castle said, 'that this interest in the criminal mind is purely academic? You haven't any particular person in mind?'

Her dark blue eyes were wide and startled for a moment: then she forced a slight laugh.

'Academic? But of course! Purely so!' Perry could almost sense her reviling herself for not having seized the opportunity to press the business with both hands. 'It's just that I sort of have — er — theories about criminals. I'd like to help them get well.'

'Why?'

'Well, isn't most of the unhappiness in the world caused by crime? Isn't it natural to want to help those who are afflicted? Just as one feels an instinctive wish to save the man or woman dying of — say cancer?'

'The man or woman dying of cancer, Mrs. Lonsdale, is an object of sympathy insofar that he or she is a victim of one of the most deadly diseases of modern times. But the criminal, who has left his or her foul imprint on an innocent victim is not deserving of either sympathy or help. That is,' — the pink finger rose adamantly — 'in the view of the public. And without public support neither a psychiatrist nor anybody else can get very far. That is why, as yet, we psychiatrists are in the minority and criminals continue to be executed instead of being turned over to us in the hope they might be cured. Without wishing to seem too blunt, Mrs. Lonsdale, I do feel that you are wasting your time. Carrying a torch for criminals won't do you any good: in fact it might do you a lot of harm. The public feeling towards the criminal, be it the murderer or petty thief, is ruthlessly, inexorably cold.'

'It's been an interesting discussion, anyway. You won't mind if I turn on the TV? I'd like to hear the 9 o'clock news.'

'By all means,' Castle snuggled down comfortably. 'Let's hear what the weather gods have to say — besides knowing what we will have to do without next.'

The news was not particularly interesting, skimming over industrial crisis, international frictions, and nationalization theories. Then came an item that made

Perry and Moira sit bolt upright in their chairs.

'It was reported this evening that as yet there are no new developments in the bottle-top murder. Richard Lane, whom the police are anxious to interview concerning his acquaintance with Joyce Kempton, the murdered woman, as yet has not been located despite an extensive search. Anybody knowing the where-abouts of this man is asked to notify the police immediately. He is described as being five feet, 10 inches tall, square-faced, dark hair and eyes. When last seen he was wearing a navy blue overcoat and soft hat . . . ' The weather forecast followed, and promised warm weather to come.

Moira switched off and Adam Castle rubbed his palms.

'Good!' he exclaimed. 'Just the sort of weather we need.'

'Well . . . ' Perry stirred and got to his feet. 'That being that I think we should have a drink. How about it, Mrs. Castle? Doctor? Care for a port, sherry? Brandy and soda — '

'I'll have port, thanks,' Castle responded. 'What about you, my dear?'

'That will suit me nicely as well,' his wife said. Perry nodded and glanced at Moira.

'This time, dearest,' he said, his voice completely firm. 'I'm not taking any excuses. You must have port with the rest of us. After all we have guests. To refuse to drink with them would be — er — treason.'

Moira raised one shoulder negatively and said nothing, but her eyes followed Perry as he went to the drinks cabinet.

'Does all this mean that you don't indulge, Mrs. Lonsdale?' Castle asked, leaning forward to knock the ashes from his pipe into the fireplace.

'I'm not very keen on it,' she confessed. 'However — rather than be branded a traitor, as my husband puts it, I'll drink.'

She glanced angrily at Perry as he returned with four filled glasses on a tray. Mrs. Castle and the psychiatrist took theirs. Moira took hers up and twirled the stem gently in her fingers. Her face looked strained.

'To good weather and may all the rain

stay in Iceland,' Perry said, raising his glass — then before any of them could drink, there was a sharp crack and Moira's glass, stem broken, fell to the floor.

'Oh!' She looked stupidly at her fingers, where blood had started to ooze from a cut. 'Just look at that!'

Perry whipped out his handkerchief and wrapped it round her first and second fingertips. She smiled woodenly.

'It simply came apart in my hand,' she said. 'I must have gripped it too hard. Of all the silly things to do! I am so sorry . . . '

'I'll fix you up,' Perry said, taking her arm. 'Excuse us for a moment, will you?'

14

There was an air of peace in the big bedroom as Perry sat smoking pensively in an easy chair. Moira was on the edge of the bed brushing her black hair with firm, smooth sweeps.

'Moira, why did you throw away your chances tonight?' Perry asked at length. 'You got Dr. Castle all warmed up and ready to answer almost anything, then you faded out like a dead battery. What happened? Did you lose your nerve?'

'I'm afraid so,' Moira admitted. 'You see, it suddenly occurred to me that he might start thinking things if I asked him to help Richard. And again, what he said earlier about criminals being deserving of their punishment rather put me off my stroke.' Moira stopped brushing her hair for a moment and reflected. Her voice was slow and thoughtful as she added: 'In spite of his geniality, I find Dr. Castle rather an inscrutable sort of person.

There are hidden depths in him. I have the idea that his carefree manner is only assumed.'

'So you've noticed it too, have you?' Perry asked moodily. 'He has the sort of look that makes you feel you are being psychoanalyzed. Since that is part of his job, I suppose one has to expect it . . . '

He strolled over to Moira and sat down beside her. 'You know,' he said, 'it was rather a startling coincidence at that.'

'Coincidence? What?'

'Our running into Castle as we did. The more I think of it, the more it puzzles me.'

'But why should it? We knew he was planning a motor trip; there wasn't anything so very remarkable about meeting him on the highway. There was no suggestion that he fixed things deliberately because the garage man told you his car was in a bad way, didn't he?'

'Yes,' Perry admitted, reflecting. 'For some reason, though, I can't quite understand it. Call me crazy if you like, but I think he perhaps engineered things with remarkable skill so we'd invite him here.'

'But why? There's no point in it. Besides, don't forget our meeting at the Metz was pure chance. What did we do or say there which would give him the sudden urge to — well, muscle in here?'

'As far as I can recall we didn't do anything. In fact, you said precious little until it occurred to you he might be able to help Richard Lane.'

Perry got to his feet, perplexity still riding his features. Hands in the pockets of his dressing gown he studied the girl.

'I'm not at all comfortable, dearest,' he said, shaking his head. 'I thought that when Chief Calthorp came here and collected all the evidence he appeared to want our part in the bottle-top murder finished. Now I begin to wonder . . . Police methods are so confoundedly subtle sometimes. They'll go to almost any length — within legal limits — to get what they want . . . '

Moira's eyes were questioning.

'If you're right,' Moira said, with a moody stare, 'what does it all mean? What does Castle want here? It's Dick Lane the police are looking for. They surely can't think he's hiding in this house?'

'Hardly — but there are other angles. Don't forget that you are one of the girls with whom Richard Lane was entangled. That makes you a star witness. There is the possibility Richard Lane may try to get at you and Castle is a kind of unofficial detective waiting to spring some kind of trap; or, more likely, he is here for a psychiatric purpose.'

Moira's face, framed by the wealth of black hair, was like a mask. Her voice was low-pitched.

'A psychiatric purpose?'

'That's right. You said yourself and you told Chief Calthorp about Lane's dislike of glass. He said himself that that took things into the realm of psychiatry. Maybe Castle was consulted and is now on the job to see what he can dig up.'

'But why out of us?'

'I don't know, unless he thinks that by studying you he may be able to find some explanation for Richard Lane's remarkable behavior. Maybe you act on Lane like a kind of mental — er — catalyst, or something.'

From irritation, Moira's expression changed to one of sheer amazement.

'A mental what?'

'Catalyst.' Perry shrugged. 'Scientifically, as I recall, it's an element that affects another element in an unpredictable way. Nobody can understand why: it just does. Maybe it happens among people. I've heard of murders being committed through clairvoyant influence. Maybe we have something similar here and Castle is anxious to get to the root of it.'

'This is too fantastic for words,' Moira scoffed. Then she grew serious again. 'Just the same, the rest of your guesses may not be so far wrong. And it worries me, Perry. It means I just dare not ask Castle now about Richard in case that's the move he is waiting for. I might get myself involved in a mass of trouble from which I shan't be able to escape. I'll have to keep quiet. ON the other hand,' — she brightened slightly — 'you may be wrong and the whole business, is coincidence after all.'

'Let's hope so anyway.'

He kissed her gently and stroked her hair.

'I just don't know how you do it,' he mused.

'Do what?'

'Fix your hair without a mirror. Come to think of it, I've never seen you look in one since we met.'

★   ★   ★

There was a letter for Moira the following morning. She saw it propped beside her plate as she entered the morning-room. It made her slow her pace unconsciously, then with a stern effort she controlled herself and smiled at Dr. Castle and his wife.

Moira recognized the writing on the cheap envelope as that of Richard Lane. The postmark was Brinhampton, 6:15 the previous evening. The letter read:

'Syl: I have got to see you, I must see you! Make it tonight at the junction of the Larches road and the main road. Say midnight. Everything will depend on it. For God's sake don't fail me. Dick.'

Moira read it again, standing motionless — then Perry's voice penetrated the veil of her preoccupation.

'Come along, dear. We want to get going soon.'

'Eh? What?' She gave a start and turned, crushing the letter in her palm. 'Oh yes, of course, I'm afraid I was wool-gathering . . . '

'Who wants to know what?' Perry inquired cheerfully, and seeing her questioning look he added. 'I mean, who was the letter from?'

'That? It — it was from Helen. She hopes we're well . . . The usual stuff.'

'And she addressed it to you and ignored me?' Perry looked amazed for a moment, then he caught a warning gleam in Moira's eyes and let the matter drop.

'Hand better, Mrs. Lonsdale?' Castle inquired pleasantly.

'Much better, thanks.'

Perry continued the conversation by suggesting they drive to Exeter, returning in the evening by a circuitous route.

'For the love of Mike what are you

looking so worried about? What's happened?' Perry asked anxiously after their guests had gone to make ready for the journey.

Moira handed him the crumpled note. He frowned as he read it.

'So he's in this district, eh? Just how can you be sure this is from him?'

'I don't think there's any doubt about it, Perry. I'd know his writing anywhere.'

'That being so, it makes everything lovely. We've got him! All we have to do is let the police know about this and they'll pick him up.'

'No, they won't!' Moira said quickly.

'What! You mean to say you won't act, now that you have the opportunity? You've got to, dearest — and you know it.'

'Dick is plainly in one of his rational moods,' she replied. 'The wording of his note shows it. He probably doesn't remember about the murders or attacking me. I must see him and find out what he wants. I owe it to him.'

'Oh, no, you don't!' Perry snapped. 'I'm your husband and I won't stand for it.'

'Please, Perry, try and understand . . . '
Moira laid her hand gently on his arm.
'You said yourself that you agree there is
a possibility Dick did not kill Joyce
Kempton, even though everything points
to it. That being the case, he might tell me
something and between us we could help
him.'

'Why should we? Hasn't he caused
enough trouble already?'

Moira waited for his anger to cool.

'You're making it hard for me, Perry,'
she said, shaking her head. 'I have loved
Dick from the moment I met him. I just
can't help it. It's something inside me.
For that reason, no matter what he may
have done or may yet do, I'm going to see
him.'

'All of which means that you married
me for protection only, eh? Just as you
told the Chief Inspector?'

'That's it,' she acknowledged quietly.
'After all, it was you who forced the pace.
I never suggested that we get married; I
fully intended to go my own way. You
came to the hotel that morning and said
you'd made up your mind to marry me

— so having no position, very little money and great need of security, I married you. I've tried hard to forget Dick and love you, Perry, but one just can't make their emotions about-face that easily.'

Perry gave a cynical grin and lit a cigarette.

'I do wish you wouldn't take it in this spirit, Perry.'

'How else do you suggest I take it? Want me to dance a hornpipe or something?'

'I married you, Perry, and I intend to remain faithful to my obligations until the end. Even if I cannot give you my love, which, after all, is something which must spring from the heart, I can give you everything else — affection, devotion, loyalty . . . '

'Well anyway,' Perry said, wearily, 'you are frank. I like that. I think we understand each other better now than at any time since we met . . . But we've wandered away from the original topic of Richard Lane.'

'I'm going to see him,' she said, with an

air of finality. 'Please don't destroy my faith in you, and perhaps his chances of giving vital information, by notifying the police.'

'You have the oddest knack of making me change my mind,' Perry said. 'All right, I'll say nothing. But I insist on going with you. You married me for protection, you say; well, you're going to get it.'

'Very well.' She seemed resigned to it. 'And of course Dr. Castle must not suspect anything. If he should, we might get into a fearful mess.'

'We'll get in one anyway if the police discover we've been obstructing them,' Perry reminded her. 'But we'll risk it.'

He got to his feet. 'We'd better get ready for the trip. Come on.'

15

The sinister, mysterious aura cast by Richard Lane was completely dispelled, at least for Perry, by the bright sunshine. Moira, too, was smiling as if she hadn't a care in the world.

Added to this was the genial banter of Dr. Castle.

'Like motoring, Mrs. Lonsdale?' the doctor asked, pleasantly.

'Why yes, I do. I think it's about one of the most enjoyable ways there is of spending the time. No effort attached, and yet you see everything. A house on wheels, in fact.'

'Yes indeed . . . ' Castle brooded over something, though his mouth was smiling. 'Some people, though merely motor because they have to, the quickest means of getting from place to place. But underneath it all they're scared to death of accidents.'

A cloud seemed to pass over Moira's features.

'I suppose I shouldn't be, but I am,' she confessed.

'Why should you be afraid?' asked Perry. 'You've never mentioned it before.'

'It's not a thing I like to talk about.'

'Concerning a car?' Castle asked casually.

'Yes. When I was a little girl my parents were killed in a motor accident. I was with them. I'll never forget it . . . But of course,' Moira continued, sighing, 'cars then were not as safe as they are now and besides, my husband is a first-class driver.'

'Where did this accident happen?' Castle inquired.

'Reading. We were living there at the time . . . '

Moira glanced ahead at the road. Dr. Castle drew a deep breath of satisfaction, pulled out his long-stemmed pipe and filled the bowl from an oilskin pouch.

'I take it, Mrs. Lonsdale, that you've changed your mind about carrying a torch for criminals?'

Moira looked at Perry, then turned to the psychiatrist again.

'That was what you suggested I do, wasn't it?'

'It was — and I'm glad you've taken my advice. At least, I am assuming that you have since you haven't mentioned criminal psychology since last night. I shall feel that my unexpected visit has been helpful, if only for that. You might have expended a good deal of energy and effort to no purpose, Mrs. Lonsdale.'

'Just the same, I don't say that I'm going to drop my studies of psychiatry and the criminal entirely,' Moira said. 'It is a topic of absorbing interest. I think it's definitely the science of the future in that it seeks to explain the working of the mind. Once we have that we know how the body works, too. Being a grosser strata, it must obey the dictates of the mind.'

Adam Castle chuckled as he lighted his pipe.

'Here we go again!' he exclaimed. 'I've rarely come across any woman — or man either — so engrossed in this business. Tell me, Mrs. Lonsdale, what do you think of environment? Do you believe that it molds the mind more completely than any other factor?'

'I'm convinced of it. I believe that nearly all the ills of the flesh — or rather, the mind — can be traced to childhood environment. In my opinion, if it were possible for every human being to be reared in beautiful surroundings, there would be no crime, no disease, no unhappy conditions.'

'Mmmm . . . ' Castle pursed his lips round his pipe. 'Unhappily it can't be done. Millions are born in squalor — and remember it. The thud of a drunkard's fist against a mother is remembered by the child for a lifetime and might easily produce a profound inhibition within the child, which only becomes apparent in adult life. The memory of imprisonment under the stairs, inside a cupboard, engenders that most common of all complaints — claustrophobia. The memory of a high building and the danger it spells to the child mind often brings on acrophobia in later years. And so it goes, right down the list. And the real trouble is that the victim is seldom aware of the reason for his condition. He puts it down to a mental impulse, which is all wrong.'

Moira considered this for a space, her forearm on the back of the seat and her chin resting on it as she absently watched the speeding countryside. The warm breeze puffed her dark hair gently.

'In spite of that, doctor,' she said, 'I have read of cases where the victim has known the reason for his condition and has tried to conquer it — and failed.'

'True,' Castle agreed. 'There are such instances.'

'What is the remedy then?'

'Now we're really diving off the top board,' Castle chuckled. 'The person who tries to destroy his or her trouble by self-analysis can rarely, if ever, succeed. The destruction of a mental flaw depends on one thing alone — its complete and ruthless exposure. And by exposure, I mean to the world at large.'

'To the world at large!' Moira looked startled. 'But in what way?'

'As a student of psychiatry, Mrs. Lonsdale, I should have thought it would have been apparent to you. Impulses — and for the sake of convenience, let us say criminal impulses — are, of course, begotten of some flaw in the working of the mind. In the vernacular it's called a 'black-out.' That is so much nonsense. Actually it is the effect of a repressed impulse. Some incident away back in the life of the person concerned has made a diabolical impression on his mind. He never speaks of it. He bottles it up inside himself and, like all unpleasant things, it grows until finally there are moments when it dominates the mind completely — and then the person sometimes performs acts similar to the one which caused the original impression . . . Do I make myself clear?'

'I think so,' Moira assented. 'For example, let us say that a very young child sees a knife gash somebody's finger. As the child matures, nursing the horrifying incident in his mind, it might at times swamp his normal will and cause him to perform an act identical to the one he originally witnessed — that is, attacking with a knife, and very probably attacking the fingers. Yet afterwards he might not be quite aware of what he had done.'

'That's the general trend of it,' Castle acknowledged. 'In fact, certain criminals have been noted for their peculiar 'characteristic' methods. Some have removed a finger from the victim for no apparent reason. Others have left a distinctive mark behind — all of which points to an underlying psychological factor.'

There was a long silence, save for the hum of the tires and the shrill of a lark overhead. Then Perry gave a low but audible whistle.

'Whew! How much will you be charging for the lecture, Dr. Castle?'

'I'm afraid I've been boring you,' he said apologetically. 'For that, though, I'm thinking you must blame your wife, Lonsdale. Once I get started, only a sledge-hammer will stop me. Just the same, I'm left with the feeling that it is a somewhat dreary topic for such a glorious day. Smell that air! Wonderful, my dear, isn't it?'

'Fortunately, Adam, your talking doesn't interfere with it,' his wife commented. 'Otherwise, I'm afraid we would all have been suffocated by now.'

It was 7 o'clock when Perry drove up the Larches.

'That,' observed Castle as he eased his great bulk out of the car, 'was one of the best days I have ever spent. And if the weather holds, there'll be more like it, eh?'

'There certainly will,' Perry promised. He waited until Mrs. Castle and Moira were out of the car and then added, 'See you in the house. I'll just garage the old tub.'

A few minutes later he hurried upstairs to change for dinner.

'I could really believe that I'm enjoying life if it were not for the thought of the confounded subterfuge we have to go through at midnight,' Perry said, as he unlaced his shoes.

'Then why come?' Moira asked. 'I'd much rather you didn't.'

'I don't think we need to go into that again, dearest.'

He hustled into the dressing-room for a shave and wash. When he returned Moira was putting on her earrings.

'I thought it was rather clever the way you pumped the old boy without giving anything away,' he commented. 'Did it give you any fresh sidelights on your beloved Richard?'

'It told me one thing which I had never quite realized — that a mental aberration has to be exposed to the world before it can be destroyed,' Moira said soberly. 'I'd never quite understood that before.'

'But if Richard Lane won't let himself be analyzed and his mental quirk, whatever it is, exposed, where do you stand?'

'As far as the psychiatric angle is concerned, I don't think I shall bother,' the girl replied. Perry glanced at her eagerly.

'Say, do you really mean that?

She nodded. 'Yes, I mean it, Perry. I'm just beginning to realize there are too many difficulties in the way. Now that I have found out that a mental kink can only be really exposed by tracing backwards into the person's history — and that an outsider has to do the tracing — I'm satisfied. I shan't question Dr. Castle any more or bring up the subject of psychiatry again. Most certainly I shan't ask him to try and save Dick. Besides, if your theory of Castle being a 'plant' is correct, the less said the better.'

'Agreed — but I suppose you're still determined to meet Lane tonight?'

'I insist on it, just in case he happens to have some information which may prove his innocence.'

Perry sighed and shrugged. 'All right, if you insist.'

Before long Moira and he were on their way downstairs. The psychiatrist was in the drawing-room, talking to his wife when they entered.

So she could keep a grip on the conversation and forestall any driftings in a psychiatric direction, Moira began talking almost immediately — chiefly on the day's trip to Exeter, the prospects of the next day's weather — in fact everything commonplace which she could call to mind . . .

It was, in fact, a species of small talk

that she maintained throughout dinner and beyond it, until at last, shortly after they had repaired to the drawing-room, Castle announced his intention of retiring.

'Fresh air's laid me low,' he grinned. When they were alone, Moira gave a little sigh of relief.

'Worked out better than I dared hope.' She glanced at her watch. 'Only half-past 9. By midnight the pair of them will be sound asleep and the coast will be clear.'

'Uh-huh,' Perry agreed moodily.

Somehow she and Perry whiled away the time — talking at intervals or else reading — until towards 11 o'clock Pearson presented himself.

'Will there be anything further, sir, or shall I lock up?'

'Before you retire,' Moira put in, 'bring coffee for both of us, please.'

'Coffee?' Perry repeated. 'What's the idea?'

'We may have a long night before us. We want to be as wide awake as possible, don't we?'

Moira poured the coffee. She said

169

nothing until they had both drained their cups, then she took Perry's and set it down beside her own on the tray.

'You still insist on coming with me?' she asked, getting to her feet and looking down on him.

'Oh, hang it all, Moira, do we have to go through all that again?'

'No, it isn't really necessary, because you're not coming with me.'

'But I am!'

She shook her dark head, felt in the pocket of her dress and held up a small bottle.

'Sleeping tablets!' he ejaculated, sitting up sharply. 'What the — !'

'I know you'll hate me for doing it, but I believe it's for the best.'

Perry was on his feet, gripping her arms and staring into her white, set face.

'Look here, Moira, what are you trying to pull off?' he demanded thickly.

'Nothing at all. It is simply that Dick would not tell me anything if you are there — and besides, I don't trust you.'

'Don't trust me?' Perry felt his head

swim a little. 'What sort of a remark is that?'

'Once you got near Dick, you might do lots of things — such as knocking him unconscious and calling the police. What could I do about it if you did? I'm not going to run that risk. I mean to see him alone.'

'All right . . . ' he whispered. 'All right! Get out! Go and see this cut-throat swine whom you love so much! If you never return I shall at least know why — '

16

Moira took the bottle of sleeping tablets out of her pocket and put it back in the medicine cupboard. For an instant as she shut the mirrored door, she caught a glimpse of her strained, resolute face and turned away sharply. Then moving to the shelf over the washbowl, she picked up a glass tumbler, put it in the inside pocket of her topcoat, then slipped the coat on. Then she glided silently down the stairs and out into the night.

She moved swiftly and was breathing hard by the time she reached the end of the lane where the main road crossed at right angles to it.

'Dick!' she called softly, looking about her in the gloom. 'Dick, are you there? It's Sylvia!'

Nothing stirred. She frowned to herself, felt in the inside pocket of her coat and pulled out the tumbler. She grasped it firmly in her right hand.

'Dick!' she repeated. 'Are you there?'

There was only the silence of the night and the soft wind blowing on her heated face. She began walking up and down with short, impatient steps. Then she halted suddenly as a low, faint whistle sounded from across the road.

'Dick! That you?'

The whistle came again in gentle response. Moira hurried towards a clump of short, thick trees.

'Dick!' she called insistently.

There was a rustling among the trees. She swung with the tumbler — then something reached out from behind and fastened under her chin. It was a powerful arm.

She struggled savagely, but to no avail. A hand crushed about her right wrist. She was forced to drop the tumbler.

To her relief, the arm about her neck was withdrawn and her hands thrust up behind her back. She stumbled and gasped with pain. Then before she realized what was happening, she was flat on her face and her assailant was crashing away through the undergrowth.

She scrambled up, breathing hard, and stared around her. The sounds were growing faint. Soon night was deadly still again.

She fingered her throat. Then she groped about on the ground for the tumbler, without success.

In a grim, troubled mood she returned to the Larches. Perry was fast asleep where she had left him.

She had only been asleep a few hours when a slight noise awakened her. It sounded like something metallic — the tapping of a spoon against the side of a cup.

She opened her eyes and saw Perry standing beside the bed, unshaven, expressionless, pale from the effects of unnatural slumber. Evidently it had been he who had drawn back the window drapes.

'Here's some tea. I know you like it and the domestics aren't up yet.'

Moira sat up, averting her eyes as she took the cup. She stirred the tea slowly.

'It is sweetened,' he said. 'And it isn't drugged, either.'

The cold note in his voice stung her for a moment. She forced her eyes to meet his and found them studying her carefully.

'I awoke about half an hour ago,' he went on, seating himself on the edge of the bed. 'Naturally my first thought was for you, though I guessed you were all right because I found your coat over me.'

'I didn't want you to catch cold,' Moira explained.

'You're one mass of contradictions, Moira. First you said last night that you didn't trust me, and drugged me because of it. Then you put a coat over me for fear I might catch cold . . . I give up!'

'I said I didn't trust you as far as Dick was concerned, and I meant it. You wouldn't have been human if you had stood aside and let him walk off — '

'Never mind that. Did you meet him? What did he say?'

Moira set the cup down. 'I don't know whether I met him or not, Perry. All I do know is that somebody whistled from that little wood at the corner of the lane and I went to answer it. The next thing I knew,

I was half strangled by an arm round my throat. After that I was flung on the ground and whoever it was dashed away.'

'Do you think murder might have been the original intention?'

'Possibly. I went prepared for it, though. I took my toothbrush tumbler.'

'A tumbler! What on earth for?'

'Well, I was going to smash it and use it as a weapon, but I didn't get the chance. It was forced out of my hand and I lost it. Whether he took it or not, or knowing what it was, was scared away, I don't know. The fact remains he ran for it and . . . I came back here.'

Perry got to his feet and rubbed his chin.

'When I came up here, I had intended to read the riot act,' he said grimly. 'But now — well, I don't think I shall. If you must know what's caused the change of heart, it's because I admire your courage. Going alone out into the night to meet a maniac and attempt to defeat him by using his own means of attack is good enough for me. And finally, since you do not intend to have anything more to do with him, there isn't much point in starting an argument.'

Moira smiled and nodded.

'All right, let's forget about the whole thing and see if we can't start off fair and square again.'

'Seem to have lost your sunburn, Lonsdale,' Dr. Castle remarked casually, during breakfast. 'Have a bad night?'

'On the contrary, doctor, I slept extremely well.'

'That's all right then. Thought you looked a bit pale. Don't mind me mentioning it; I'm accustomed to noting people's complexions — and reactions.'

'Where are we going today, Mr. Lonsdale?' Mrs. Castle inquired. 'Have you any particular place in mind?'

'As a matter of fact I — '

Perry broke off as a loud knock sounded on the front door. Pearson hurried out of the room. ' — matter of fact I haven't,' Perry finished absently. His eyes strayed to Moira. She flashed him a quick, meaning glance. Both of them knew that only one man made a noise like that on the front door

— Inspector Chanworthy. And if Pearson came in and announced him, with the psychiatrist here, whom they both wanted to sidetrack as much as possible — !

Pearson entered and cleared his throat. 'There's — '

'Yes, Pearson, I'll come,' Perry said hurriedly. 'I know who it is . . . '

Feeling suddenly warm, he hurried from the room and came to a stop in the hall. But it was not Inspector Chanworthy. Chief Inspector Calthorp and Sergeant Dixon were waiting, hats in hand.

Perry closed the door and smiled feebly.

'Well, Inspector, back again! How are you?'

'Good morning, sir. I've some good news for you and your wife. Perhaps you wouldn't mind telling her that I'm here?'

'Good news?' Perry's face brightened. 'Why, yes, certainly I'll tell her. Excuse me.'

He glanced into the morning-room, caught Moira's eye and moved his head slowly. She came out. Perry led the way to the library.

'We've got Richard Lane,' Calthorp announced casually.

'You have?' Moira's voice was steady. 'May I ask where and how, or is it an official secret?'

'Secret? Why, no. He was caught early this morning trying to board a London train at Brinhampton station. He's now in custody, so whatever worries you may have had regarding him making another attack on you, Mrs. Lonsdale, can now be dispelled.'

'Yes . . . it's a big relief,' Moira murmured absently, then gave the inspector a searching look. 'Did he say anything? Admit anything?'

'Well, no . . . ' Calthorp reflected for a moment. 'That is, not in connection with the murder of Joyce Kempton or the attack on Miss Ransome — but he did say he had tried to get in touch with you and had written a letter. What is more, he said that you answered it in person, last night . . . That he met you. Is that correct?'

'I'm afraid it is,' Moira said uneasily.

'I'd like you to tell me about it. I must

have all the facts.'

Moira did so and Calthorp listened attentively, his keen eyes never once leaving her face.

'Well, Mrs. Lonsdale, you behaved very badly as far as the law is concerned. You should have notified the police the moment you received the letter.'

'For some reason,' Moira said, 'I got the impression that it was not Lane who attacked me. It seemed like a much stronger man.'

'Not very likely to be anybody else, was it?' Calthorp asked coldly. 'Only Richard Lane wrote to you and only Richard Lane could have met you. I think that is more or less conclusive. As for your action in obstructing the police, I shall have to think it over. Taking the circumstances into consideration I'll see if we can't waive it this once . . . '

Waive it? Perry frowned. This was generosity to the point of incredibility. Something, somewhere, didn't tie in.

'Well, that's all I came for — to advise you how things are,' Calthorp added. 'I was in the district — since Lane was taken to the local police station — so I thought I'd call personally. Of course, you will be called later as a witness at the inquest and trial. So . . . Good morning, Mrs. Lonsdale, Mr. Lonsdale. And let me warn you against trying to obstruct the law in the future. You might not get away with it so easily again.'

He nodded to Sergeant Dixon and they went out into the hall together, Perry and Moira following behind. But before they reached the front door, Dr. Castle emerged from the morning-room. When he caught sight of Calthorp, he started.

'Well, bless my soul if it isn't Calthorp! What in the world are you doing here?'

A puzzled look crossed Calthorp's thin features.

'If it comes to that, doctor, I might ask you the same question. Or are you a friend of Mr. and Mrs. Lonsdale?'

'A very good friend of theirs, I hope! They're Good Samaritans, both of 'em. My car broke down, Mr. and Mrs. Lonsdale came across my wife and I, saw our distress, rescued us — and now we're staying here until the car's repaired.'

'Oh . . . I see.' Calthorp hesitated, then smiled. 'I just had a few words to exchange with Mr. and Mrs. Lonsdale. See you again some time, doctor.'

When the front door closed, Perry was frowning to himself and his lips were compressed. Moira was hesitating, clearly uncertain as to what she should say or do.

'Well, your bit of business being over, do we get on our way?' Castle inquired. 'That is, when we know where we're going . . . My wife and I are ready when you are.'

'Before we go,' Perry said quietly, 'I think we ought to explain things. It's obvious that you must be wondering why Calthorp was here. You don't find men in his position dropping in without good reason.'

'Oh, true.' The psychiatrist grinned pleasantly. 'But after all it's your own affair, isn't it? It has nothing to do with me. I'm simply a guest.'

'But not an ordinary one, doctor. It's quite apparent Calthorp knows you well.'

'True — and I know him well, too, together with several other of the top men in the C.I.D. At times I have even given them the benefit of my knowledge ... But that doesn't mean that you have to explain yourself. Unless of course,' Castle added dryly, 'you feel you would like to tell me about Richard Lane.'

Perry started and his eyes caught Moira's surprised expression. The psychiatrist considered them in faint amusement, chubby hands thrust in his jacket pockets.

'How on earth did you know it concerned Lane?' Moira asked.

'Oh, there's no magic in it, Mrs. Lonsdale. It is well known — for all the world to read, and hear — that Chief Calthorp is in charge of the bottle-top murder case, and that his main worry was finding Richard Lane, the probable murderer. Added to that was your own extraordinary attention to the radio the other night, Mrs. Lonsdale, when the latest news of the crime was given in the news.'

'I should have remembered that you are accustomed to reading people,' Moira said, with a faintly regretful smile.

'I assume,' Castle went on, 'that your intense interest in psychiatry, Mrs. Lonsdale, is motivated by one thing alone — your connection with Richard Lane. That you have a connection has just become apparent, otherwise Calthorp would not have called.'

'Calthorp came to tell us that Lane has been arrested,' Perry said quietly. 'They caught him at the railway station last night.'

Castle made no comment; merely nodded his silvery head interestedly.

17

Moira was surprised to discover how much she now hated this immense, genial man. It was his extreme cordiality that she distrusted. And it had been a shock to learn how much he already knew.

With these thoughts in mind Moira did not look particularly happy as she got in the car beside Perry. He glanced at her, but made no comment.

'Not feeling well, Mrs. Lonsdale? Sun too hot for you, perhaps?'

'Too hot? Why, no, I'm feeling fine.' She moved irritably. 'Why is it that when you want to be quiet, somebody always wonders if you're ill, bad-tempered, or dying on your feet?'

'Thinking isn't always good for the constitution,' Castle reminded her. 'Depending, of course, upon the nature of the thoughts. We should all be very careful what we think about if we wish to remain healthy.'

'Delightfully vague, doctor, if I may say so,' Moira commented acidly.

He sat back and filled his pipe slowly, his eyes on the back of the girl's neck.

'There isn't much you can do for Richard Lane, you know,' he said. 'So why torture your mind trying to think of something?'

Moira turned to him quickly. 'Apparently you are something more than just a psychiatrist, Dr. Castle! A mind-reader, as well, it seems.'

'Not I,' he chuckled. 'I'm a student of moods, that's all. Yesterday you were as bright as a lark; today you are as moody as can be. Only one thing, to my knowledge, has come in between — Inspector Calthorp. He, in turn, suggests Richard Lane. You have spoken almost ceaselessly about the criminal mind, and I have answered most of your questions . . . Richard Lane has been captured. That leaves little else to occupy your thoughts. I'm right, Mrs. Lonsdale, am I not?'

'Yes, dead right,' Perry interrupted tartly. 'There's no sense in beating about the bush. My wife should realize that she can't pull wool over your eyes — of all people.'

Moira gave Perry a long, bitter look that startled him. Then she turned to consider Castle.

'My husband's quite correct in what he says,' she admitted. 'And he's also probably right when he says there's no point in beating about the bush.'

'I'm not inquisitive, you know,' Castle assured her. 'I just wondered if perhaps I could help you, that's all.'

'What did you mean by saying there isn't much I can do for Richard Lane? There might be.'

'As I see it, from what you've told me, you believe there may be a psychological reason for Richard Lane's actions, that he murdered Joyce Kempton because of some queer mental impulse. What impulse exactly? Have you any idea? If you have, we might edge a bit nearer the truth.'

'I suppose,' Moira sighed, 'I may as well explain and let you make what you can of it . . . I know of only two significant things about Richard Lane. In the normal way he is a real decent chap. But he has one strange characteristic. He's afraid of glass. It does things to him, broken glass especially. That, I think, is the reason why he attacked Joyce Kempton with a broken bottle.'

'Is anyone else aware of this trait besides you?'

'There may be others, but perhaps they haven't attached any importance to it. In fact, from what I've read of the case in the newspapers, nobody else seems to have come forward and said anything about him — either for or against.'

'And what,' Adam Castle asked, 'is your connection with him, Mrs. Lonsdale?'

'He was my . . . Well, my boy friend. Until I met Mr. Lonsdale.'

'I see. Then what connection was there between Joyce Kempton and him?'

'Also a girl friend.'

'He had two, eh?' Castle raised his eyebrows and puffed hard at his pipe. 'My word, obviously a man of courage. But, Mrs. Lonsdale, it seems a long jump from Richard Lane to Mr. Lonsdale here. Can't you fill in the blanks for me?'

'I'll do my best,' Moira volunteered, and repeated the story she had given Chief Inspector Calthorp. The end of the narrative left Castle brooding and tugging at his pipe.

'There doesn't seem to me to be much you can do to help him,' he said finally. 'Basing his homicidal impulses on crystalophobia never would convince a jury, even though from the psychiatric angle it might be shown that for some reason glass has a peculiar effect on his mind. Certainly you yourself would not get much of a hearing because you deliberately withheld the truth from the police — not once, but twice. The first time when you saw him leaving Joyce Kempton's rooming-house, and the second when you received a letter from him yesterday morning. Those incidents would be taken into account in assessing the value of your evidence, you know.'

'Do you believe, then, that he will be convicted and hanged?'

'Unless something vital can nullify the evidence against him, I'm certain of it. And I warn you, Mrs. Lonsdale, that you're likely to come in for some severe censure.'

'Yes, I suppose so,' she muttered. 'I can stand that, though. How long do you think it will be before he's brought to trial?'

'It will be the summer assizes in May. Couple of months yet. You'll have plenty of time to decide your course of action.'

'I don't think so,' Moira answered, shaking her head. 'Since I can't do anything about the mental kink, I'll simply fill the role of an ordinary witness and speak the truth. Let the law take its course. I'd only get myself into a worse mess, I suppose, trying to protect a homicidal maniac. As I said to my husband this morning, it will be better for both of us if we look upon it as though Dick Lane doesn't exist any more.'

Adam Castle jabbed a thumb into the bowl of his pipe.

'It's more than likely there will be a psychiatrist in court anyway,' he said. 'Sometimes he is referred to as a medical expert, but his actual job is to judge from the answers of the prisoner what sort of a mind he has. The same thing may be said of some of the witnesses — to determine if they are speaking the truth or if — unconsciously maybe — they are withholding something.'

Moira's face went blank. 'But I never knew they did that sort of thing at a trial!'

'Consider it a behind-the-scenes tip,' Castle said, smiling. 'I've had that role myself on occasion. I remember one instance where a witness had to submit to the Rohrsach test. In case you are not conversant with it, it is an ink blot which, when enlarged, photographed and shown to the person, indicates his or her mental trend.'

'The — Rohrsach test . . . ' Moira repeated the words slowly and then shook her head. 'No. I never heard of it.'

'I'll demonstrate it to you when we get back home.'

'No . . . No, there's really no need.' Moira set her mouth. 'I'd much rather forget all about the business.'

They stopped in Dorchester for lunch and Moira became quite talkative — even genial. Her voice had a superficial, brittle ring, however, which Perry was not slow to notice. Maybe Castle noticed it, too, but he made no comment. In fact, for most of the afternoon, as the car glided easily through Beaminster, Crewkerne and then out to Yeovil, he was in his habitual mood of complete bonhomie . . .

Gradually, Perry headed back towards Taunton and Brinhampton . . . and the Larches. They arrived at almost the same time as on the previous evening. Their actions, too, were similar. After Perry put the car in the garage, Moira, the psychiatrist and his wife, had climbed out. When he entered the house he went straight upstairs to change for dinner.

The only difference, this time, was that whereas he had opened the conversation the previous evening, it was Moira who did it this time — bitterly, sharply, as if prompted by an uncontrollable emotion.

'Perry, I'm getting sick of having that old fool tacked on to us.'

'Huh?' He looked at her in surprise. 'Of Dr. Castle? Why, what's he done? He strikes me as being the best company we've ever had around these parts.'

'He's too complacent, too sure of himself. In fact,' Moira finished, 'I think it's about time he went. We can't even get a moment to ourselves.'

'You're exaggerating a bit, aren't you?' Perry asked quietly. 'And even if we did have a lot of time to ourselves, what good would it do us? You'd sit and brood over that infernal Richard Lane, and I'd sulk because of it. I think that with our kind of bargain — since love doesn't seem to enter into it as far as you're concerned — it's the best thing that could happen for us to have congenial company. It keeps us civil and up to scratch.'

'That was the way things were before Richard was caught,' Moira said. 'It's all changed now. Since he's in prison, he's no longer a threat over our heads. I feel that I can really expand — do things — act freely. Then I think of that fat old man sitting around, smiling, watching, probing . . . ' Her dark eyes flamed for a moment. 'And it makes me feel as if I'd like to scream.'

'If we are to behave with even a semblance of courtesy we can't get rid of him until his car is fixed.'

'I think we can,' Moira retorted. 'And if — as I still inwardly believe — he is connected with Scotland Yard and is only here for what he can discover, it will serve him right to get pitched out. We'll go to the south of France and shut the place up. Then he'll just have to go.'

'Yes, but . . . ' Perry looked uneasy. 'It'll seem like a rather sudden decision, won't it?'

'Why should it? We told him our honeymoon was only postponed. We can also tell him that now Dick's disposed of, we've decided to take our honeymoon as planned.'

'And I know what his answer to that one will be — that we are not supposed to leave the country when we may be called as witnesses.'

'But that's two months away — in May. Dr. Castle said so himself.'

'That may be, but don't you realize we may be interviewed a lot before then? If you think we've seen the last of our frosty friend, Inspector Calthorp, I don't. Most certainly you haven't. You're the star witness. That is what I keep trying to impress upon you.'

'Yes, I suppose you're right,' she said thoughtfully. 'Well, that leaves only one alternative. We'll close up the place, just the same, and go to the flat in London. We can have plenty of fun in there, and it will have the desired effect of getting rid of Castle. He certainly won't want to be in London with us when his own home's there — and anyway, there wouldn't be room in the flat.' Her eyes brightened. 'Yes, Perry, that's it. And entirely logical too.'

'Nothing wrong with it,' he agreed, 'but I can't help wondering at your sudden dislike of our tubby friend. As far as I can see, he's done nothing except help you and hand out information for which normally he would charge a fee. And besides, what's happened to your original notion about taking him to try and sort out Richard Lane's mental difficulties? That was your prime reason for cultivating his acquaintance in the first place, wasn't it?'

'That was before it had occurred to either of us that he might be connected with Scotland Yard. Besides, you heard what he said in the car today — that I'm wasting my time. Since that is so, Castle becomes superfluous — and we're going to London if only to get rid of him.'

'All right, Moira, but you can do your own dirty work. I just haven't enough nerve to tell him he's being kicked out — and that is what it really amounts to. We are supposed to have several more days' touring to get through, don't forget.'

'Touring.' Moira gazed at the ceiling hopelessly. 'I just couldn't stand another minute of it — not with Castle in the back staring at my neck. I can feel him doing it and it gives me the creeps.'

Perry grinned and went into the dressing-room. He shaved and washed and came back with a towel around his neck. Moira was lounging against the end of the bed, wrapped in thought.

'Perry . . . '

'Yes, what?' He removed the towel and tossed it to one side.

'You say you've got a lot of money and influence?'

'Sure — bags of both.' He looked puzzled. 'What about it? Want me to write a check?'

'No — but I was thinking you might be able to use both your money and influence to help me disappear.'

Perry stared stupidly at his reflection in the mirror.

'Help you to do what?'

'London,' Moira said, with a smile, 'is such a huge place — so easy to vanish in it. I don't see why it couldn't be managed.'

Perry walked over to her.

'What crazy sort of scheme have you got on your mind now?' he snapped. 'Disappear indeed! Why in the world should you want to do that?'

'So I couldn't be called as a witness at the trial. Once I get in that court, I'll have to swear on oath to speak the whole truth — and I can't do it, Perry. I just can't — because every word I shall have to say will condemn Dick to death. The only way out is to vanish.'

'But even if you did run away and hide

— which is about the wildest idea I ever heard of — it wouldn't do you any good,' said Perry. 'You made your statement to Calthorp before witnesses, don't forget, and Sergeant Dixon took down everything in shorthand. Shortly no doubt, that statement will be brought to you to sign. Your evidence would be read even in your absence — so you see, there is actually no way out.'

Perry grasped her shoulder gently and smiled.

'Forget such an idea, dearest. I know how you feel, but I'm certainly not going to help you do a thing like that. You will face up in court just as I shall, as my wife. You don't think I'm going to have it plastered all over the town that my wife has vanished, do you?'

'Does that mean at root that you're thinking more of your personal prestige than my feelings?'

'Oh, don't be so difficult, Moira.' Perry glared at her. 'Behave as though you're grown up. People can't just disappear in the casual manner you suggest — not people who count, anyway. And you certainly do, being Mrs. Perry Lonsdale.'

18

True to his promise that he was not going to do any of the 'dirty work' himself Perry confined his conversation to everyday topics as he met the exchanges of Dr. Castle and his wife across the table. When the meal was half over, Moira took advantage of a lull.

'I don't quite know how you're going to take this, Dr. Castle, but we've decided to close the Larches and return to London — to our flat. We have one there, you know.'

'So you mentioned,' Castle replied genially. 'But why should it matter how I take it? I think you're being very sensible. After dinner I'll ring up the nearest hotel and book rooms to start from tomorrow. I take it you won't be going until then?'

'No — tomorrow morning.'

'Good.'

When dinner was over, Castle went to the telephone and arranged for rooms at the Roseleaf hotel in Suttonmear, 10 miles away. Then he went into the drawing-room. His wife was talking with Perry, and Moira was glancing through the evening paper.

'That's funny,' she exclaimed presently.

'What?' Perry asked.

'Not a word about Richard Lane's arrest.'

'It is a bit strange,' Perry agreed.

'There must be a good reason for it.' Castle interjected. 'Leave it to Calthorp; he knows what he's doing.'

After breakfast the following morning, the Castles departed.

'That finishes that, anyway!' Moira exclaimed as they drove away with Pearson at the wheel.

'Maybe you had the right idea at that,' Perry agreed. He rubbed his hands vigorously. 'Well, we're all set to go ourselves. Nothing to do but get out the roadster and bring the bags downstairs.'

'You fixed things up with Pearson and Mrs. Carter?'

'Uh-huh. Gave each a month's vacation with pay. Pearson will bring back the other car and lock up.'

'I was just thinking about Pearson. I wonder if Inspector Calthorp ever did question him? That drugged coffee we had hasn't been explained yet. I suppose we can trust Pearson to send the key on to us?'

'It wouldn't do him any good to keep it. If he stole the car or anything from the house, the insurance would cover it — and the police would nail him in double quick time. Incidentally, I telephoned Scotland Yard and left a message for Calthorp telling him what we plan to do.'

Moira started. 'You did! What in the world for?'

'Simply to keep things straight. It's our duty to inform the police of our whereabouts.'

Moira nodded, but said nothing.

They reached their London flat shortly after 3 o'clock.

'I'll nip out and get a few things in,' said Moira. 'Won't take me above half an hour.'

'Okay. I'll sort out the luggage,' said Perry.

Moira passed several grocery stores and never even gave them a glance. She was searching for a different kind of shop entirely, and presently found it — a theatrical costumier. She paused and looked in the window. She turned to enter then paused, staring incredulously. Not very far away a man was standing, watching her. Richard Lane!

When she reached the spot in the crowd where he had been standing, there was no trace of him.

The persistent thought of an illusion beat through her brain, but commonsense insisted it had not been an illusion. It had been Richard Lane! She looked at her watch. It was 4 o'clock. She walked up the street and got on a bus. Fifteen minutes later she entered the office of Chief Inspector Calthorp at Scotland Yard.

'Well, Mrs. Lonsdale, I hardly expected to see you here,' Calthorp said pleasantly. 'Got some news for me?'

'I certainly have, inspector. I've just seen Richard Lane!'

The chief inspector looked at her curiously.

'But that's impossible. He's in custody.'

'I saw him on Chandos Street less than half an hour ago.' Moira insisted. 'He was amongst the afternoon crowds — and he was watching me.'

Calthorp snapped a switch on the interphone box.

'Get me Superintendent Lovell,' he instructed.

Calthorp rubbed his pointed chin, then he switched on again as the panel buzzed.

'Lovell?' he asked. 'Calthorp. Have you still got Richard Lane in custody?'

'Still got him, sir?' the voice echoed in surprise. 'Yes, of course.'

'All right, thanks. That's all.'

Calthorp looked at the baffled Moira across the desk.

'I am afraid your imagination has been playing you tricks,' Mrs. Lonsdale. 'Lane is safely tucked away and you can be quite sure he won't escape without our knowledge.'

With an effort, Moira forced the profound mystery into the back of her mind.

'While I am here, inspector, there's

something I'd like to ask you. Why was there nothing in the papers about Lane's arrest?'

'I had my reasons for that, Mrs. Lonsdale, but I am not at liberty to reveal them.'

Rebuffed, Moira gave a little shrug, excused herself and left the office.

By the time she reached the costumier's shop, it was closed. Moira hesitated, then went on to a grocery store and bought some provisions. Arriving home, she found Perry meticulously shaven, and wearing full dress.

'Well, what happened to you?' he demanded, taking her parcels.

'I took such a long time,' Moira said slowly, 'because I went to Scotland Yard.' Then she told him what had transpired.

'You're just a bit overwrought,' Perry said. 'You simply saw somebody who looked like Dick Lane and your imagination did the rest.'

'Yes, I suppose that's the truth,' Moira said.

They had dinner at the Metz, and left for home around midnight.

'Perry . . . ' Moira's voice came out of the gloom of the roadster.

'Well?'

'If anything should ever happen to me . . . would you be sorry?'

Perry glanced at her curiously. She was sprawled in the bucket-seat beside him, only visible at intervals as they passed under the street lamps. She seemed to be gazing straight before her, lost in thought.

'What a question!' he exclaimed, laughing gently. 'Of course I'd be sorry. What do you take me for? You're my wife, aren't you?'

'Yes — but we did agree that we hadn't really married for love after all.'

'Maybe you didn't, but in spite of all I said, I did. I naturally felt bitter when you admitted you loved Dick Lane and not me — but bitterness can be short-lived. In spite of everything — in spite of all your queer little ways and unexplained foibles — I do love you, Moira. That's why I married you.'

The next morning after breakfast they had a surprise. The bell rang and Dr. Castle stood framed in the doorway.

'Hello there, Lonsdale,' he greeted, holding out a plump hand. 'I thought I'd give you a call since you said you were coming into town.'

Perry smiled. 'Glad to see you, doctor.' He closed the door. 'But what happened to your motor trip?'

'I've cancelled it.' Castle grinned widely. 'Chiefly because the car's still off the road. Since I'm still on vacation, I thought I'd pop in and see how you're getting along.'

'Well, we're glad to see . . . '

Perry stopped and glanced round as Moira came out of the living-room.

'Dr. Castle! This is a surprise.' She shook hands. 'What brings you back to the city — business?'

'I wondered,' Castle said, 'if you'd allow me to repay you for your kindness up in Somerset . . . '

Perry laughed and shook his head. 'I won't hear of it. It was a pleasure.'

'Naturally,' Castle added, 'I don't mean in money. Would you both come to dinner and a show with my wife and me tonight?'

Perry gave Moira a glance, and she was nodding her dark head eagerly. Castle glanced at her and his smile widened a little.

'You seem to have bucked up quite a deal since you came to the city, Mrs. Lonsdale. I'm glad to see it; you were far too moody for a woman of your age . . . It comes from the heart, I suppose?'

'From the heart?'

'I may be wrong, but it seems to me your manner is somehow . . . forced. An act, to be precise. That you don't really feel as happy as you pretend.' Castle's smile faded. 'Never play tricks with yourself, Mrs. Lonsdale. It's a fatal mistake, and it twists the mind dreadfully in the long run to try and make yourself believe in something you really mistrust.'

Moira laughed softly.

'I do believe we're getting into one of those psychiatric inquisitions again, doctor. Better watch yourself, your wife isn't here to put the brakes on.'

Castle chuckled. 'Yes, I'd better. Well, I didn't come here to upset your morning's arrangements. Now I have said my little piece, I'll be on my way. Bye for now; I'll see you later.'

He went off down the corridor and Perry shut the door. He glanced at Moira and smiled.

'That settles that,' he said, shrugging. 'Can't see why you ever disliked the old boy.'

'He's all right when he doesn't live on the premises,' Moira said.

Perry and Moira were ready and waiting when the psychiatrist called at 6.30 p.m. in a taxi.

'Good,' he pronounced, when they were seated in the vehicle and the imperturbable Mrs. Castle had exchanged greetings. 'Everything going like clockwork; that's the way I like it. Incidentally,' he added, 'I didn't order wine or champagne. I know you don't care for it, Mrs. Lonsdale, nor does my wife, particularly. You, Lonsdale, can order separately if you wish. Thought I'd mention it. I don't want you to think me remiss as a host.'

'I never saw a man who looked more like one,' Perry laughed.

Moira's cheerful mood of the previous evening had returned. For this reason Perry could not help wondering why, at times, he caught the psychiatrist staring at her pensively.

'Now,' Castle said, beaming and rubbing his fat hands, 'what do you think of my arrangements? Pretty good, eh?'

'Couldn't be better,' Perry agreed.

'I ordered coffee,' Castle remarked, quite unconscious of the earthy touch he had introduced. 'If you decide to have a he-man's drink, Lonsdale — '

'Not a bit, doctor. I've done little else but drink coffee ever since Moira and I were married — '

Perry broke off and looked at the girl in surprise as a little gasp escaped her. Following her line of vision, Perry saw three people leaving a distant table — two men and a woman.

'What's the matter?' he asked curiously.

'It's — it's Dick!' Moira gasped, rising hurriedly to her feet. 'The taller one, with the dark hair.'

She hurried across the dining-room,

but they had left the building when she arrived.

Moira came back slowly. She sank into her chair, a little breathless, face deathly white.

'I — I was too late,' she whispered, gazing about the cafe with troubled eyes. 'He'd gone.'

'If I may be forgiven,' Castle remarked mildly, 'who was he? An old friend of yours, perhaps?'

'It was Richard Lane,' Moira said, turning to him sharply.

Castle, who had half raised his soup spoon, set it down again.

'Richard Lane? Oh, come now, Mrs. Lonsdale, that's impossible. He's in custody.'

'I think it's about time there was a stop to this tomfoolery,' Perry snapped.

'Look here — ' Moira began.

'A moment,' Castle murmured, raising a placating hand. 'Don't allow your tempers to get out of hand; doesn't do the constitution any good ... Mrs. Lonsdale, if you feel so sure it was Richard Lane, why don't you get in touch with Chief Inspector Calthorp?'

'I tried that yesterday. Inspector Calthorp proved — to his own satisfaction, if not to mine, that Dick Lane was in custody at the time I saw him on Chandos Street. It either means that Dick has an identical twin wandering about London, who by chance or design keeps catching my eye, or else I'm — I'm seeing things. And I'm hardly the type to do that.'

'Oh, I don't know . . . ' Castle smiled and went on with his soup.

'What did you mean, doctor — 'I don't know?' ' she asked presently. 'Do I strike you as being the kind of woman who'd see things which don't exist?'

'It is possible that the emotional condition you have created for yourself, because of your early attachment to Richard Lane, has caused your present — er — penchant for mistaken identity,' Castle replied. 'He is, as we say vulgarly, 'on your mind.' I would suggest you try shutting him out of your mind completely — and when you see somebody with similar features and attire, just keep a firm hold on your mental reactions. See that person as he is, not as you think he is.'

'And supposing I can't manage to do that?'

'In that case, I am very much afraid I may find another patient — and that's the last thing I want. Not because I'm unwilling to extend my practice, but because a little effort of will on your part can easily overcome the difficulty.'

'It's good to hear such plain common-sense, doctor,' Perry remarked, giving Moira a grim glance. 'Thanks — and I'd like to apologize for upsetting your arrangements with such nonsense.'

'Imagination isn't such nonsense as you seem to think, Lonsdale,' Castle told him seriously. 'It can drive one to very great depths, as well as to great heights.'

19

When they reached the reserved box at the Royalty, Moira deported herself in every way as became a guest. In spite of herself, she forgot her troubles in laughing at the comedian and held her breath at the balancing wizard on six tables and a chair, unaware that Dr. Castle was watching her closely.

'I do believe, Dr. Castle, that this evening is doing more than anything so far to cheer me up,' she declared. 'I really am grateful to you.'

'Oh, that's all right,' he responded, beaming. 'It is hardly coincidental that I have some slight knowledge as to the best treatment for different temperaments. Oh, any of you care for an ice?'

'I'd love one — ' Moira stopped. Her eyes were fixed on a man's face. He was at the end of the third row of stalls from the front. He glanced up and their eyes met.

Hardly conscious of what she was doing, Moira got to her feet. She flung out her hand over the plush edge of the box and pointed steadily.

'Moira!' Perry gasped, seizing her. 'Moira, what are you doing?'

'It's — it's Dick Lane!' she cried hoarsely — then everything went black.

'Give her some brandy, Lonsdale,' said Castle.

Moira felt her head and shoulders raised, then as the glass touched her lips she shot up her right hand and sent it flying. She opened her eyes and looked about her. The fallen glass was lying on the thick carpet.

'I — I didn't mean to do that,' she murmured, and stirred wearily.

By degrees it dawned on her that she was lying on a couch in the corridor. Castle was seated beside her. Standing regarding her was Perry, his face set and troubled. Mrs. Castle was standing, too, as impassive as ever; and there was also a tall, dark-haired man —

Moira gave a violent start as she saw him. 'Who — are you?' she demanded.

'My name is Gerald Cavendish,' he answered quietly.

'The gentleman you mistook for Richard Lane,' Perry explained. 'He was kind enough to come upstairs to see what was wrong. Now you can see him clearly. I hope you realize what an error you made.'

'If I've done all that is necessary,' Cavendish remarked, 'I'll get back and see the show.'

'By all means, sir,' Castle assented, glancing up. 'And many thanks for being so co-operative.'

'I just don't know what to say about this disgraceful exhibition, doctor,' Perry said, his voice taut.

The psychiatrist glanced at him soberly. For once the beaming smile was absent. The mouth was firmly set.

'You're being a bit nasty, my boy,' he said quietly. 'Your wife is anything but well — mentally, that is.' He glanced at Moira. 'You would prefer me to speak openly, I think?'

She was silent, looking as though she were struggling to understand him.

'These two incidents in the space of one evening have convinced me, Mrs. Lonsdale, that in regard to Richard Lane you have formed a phobia. Despite what things have been said to the contrary, the fact is that you detest him perhaps more than anybody else on earth!'

'No!' Moira exclaimed. 'I — I don't. I love him.'

'Why not hear me out?' Castle suggested patiently. 'You loved him once, yes; but then something happened. Your picture of a quiet, pleasant man was utterly shattered by the discovery that he was a murderer. You may not have felt any actual physical or mental shock at the time, but you received one just the same. It threw your brain a trifle out of balance. Thus you believe you see him where in truth he does not exist. The whole thing is easily explainable as latent shock.'

Moira was silent, watching, watching the psychiatrist's round, grave face.

'What's the remedy,' doctor?' Perry asked anxiously.

'What she needs is rest, quiet, a chance to think and discipline her thoughts.'

216

'By that,' Perry remarked, 'I suppose you're suggesting we should return to the Larches?'

'Yes,' Castle got to his feet. 'I am. I think it would be a very good idea if you were to return there, Mrs. Lonsdale, and avoid all excitements. I'm speaking professionally now; you've become one of my patients. I'll make arrangements for a taxi right away . . . '

★   ★   ★

They returned to the flat about 10 o'clock and were seated before the fireplace in the living-room with coffee and sandwiches when Perry put his thoughts into words.

'I'm sick and tired of having our lives messed up by this maniac Richard Lane,' he declared, 'and what's more, I'm not going to risk any more outbursts on your part.'

Moira gave a weary smile. 'What are you going to do?'

'When you have recovered from your mental upsets — and we'll let Dr. Castle be the judge of that — I think we should be divorced.'

Moira drank her coffee slowly and then set the cup down on the little table.

'All this,' she said, her voice quiet, 'has quite a strange ring after you saying you loved me so much.'

'I do love you. Nothing has changed that — but a man in my position can't even afford to let love mess up his niche in the social and financial world.'

'In other words, power and money and your shipping line above all else?'

'Since you put it that way, yes!' Perry assented, ruthlessly.

Moira got to her feet and raised and lowered a shoulder briefly.

'All right, Perry, the joy-ride's finished. I'll go back to the Larches tomorrow, collect my things, and the rest can be handled through your lawyer.'

'It doesn't have to be that sudden, Moira — '

'I think it does,' she interrupted. 'Now, if you have no objections I'll try and get some sleep. I've had more than enough for one day.'

She left the room, closing the door emphatically. Perry gave it a morose glance, then digging his hands into his trousers pockets, gave himself up to moody speculations.

By 10 o'clock next morning they were on the road to Somerset.

'I suppose,' Perry said, after a long interval of quiet, 'I'd better advise Pearson and Mrs. Carter that I'll want them to come back . . . '

'Up to you,' Moira responded. 'It won't concern me, will it? I shall be leaving tomorrow.'

'I don't see why you couldn't have stayed in London and I could have sent your things on to you,' Perry remarked. 'Or, I'd have brought them myself for that matter. And why bother about an hotel reservation? Stay at the flat. I'll not come bothering you if that's what is worrying you.'

'No.' She shook her head adamantly. 'I intend to cut myself entirely free. As for returning to the Larches, I prefer to do so because I want to make sure I get everything — including my books.'

'Oh, those things!' Perry's voice was contemptuous. 'It seems to me that they're partly to blame for everything that has happened! If you hadn't tried to figure out how to cure Richard Lane's mental kink, we wouldn't be in the mess we're in now.' Moira tightened her lips but did not respond.

'Here's the key,' Perry said, handing it across as they arrived at the Larches. 'I'll take care of the bags.'

It struck her as she opened the front door what a vast, gloomy place the Larches really was.

Her first move was to the bedroom where she rid herself of hat and coat; then she returned downstairs just as Perry came in with the bags. Perforce they had to pass each other in the hall.

'I'll see if there's anything in the kitchen worth eating,' Moira said.

The search produced only canned food, which she made into the inevitable sandwiches, and coffee. She took them into the drawing-room on the tea-trolley.

When they had finished, Perry cleared away the dishes and washed up, while

Moira collected her belongings.

'I'll leave first thing tomorrow. By train,' she announced, when her task was finished.

'Very well, if that's how you want it. Have you made your hotel reservation?'

'Yes,' Moira lied. 'The Agincourt.' Perry turned to the massive coal scuttle.

'Have to get some coal,' he said briefly, and rose.

Moira watched him go from the room, the firelight making his tall, thin figure cast a monstrous shadow on the ceiling. Then the darkness swallowed him and there was the click of the door-latch.

Moira frowned and glanced towards the closed door and listened intently. There were no sounds to indicate Perry might be breaking coal.

A sharp rap on the French window startled her. She glanced towards it, but though the drapes were drawn back, could see nothing. Perhaps it had been a low-flying bird. Perhaps —

It came again, more insistently this time, a decisive rap. And again she peered into the night, without avail. Maybe Perry had left the basement by the outside door. Moira snapped back the catch and gazed out into the night.

'That you, Perry?' she called sharply.

There were movements in the flower-bed — then Moira found herself suddenly pushed back into the room. She regained her balance and stared at the tall stranger in soft hat and overcoat.

It was Richard Lane.

'Good evening, Sylvia' he said. His voice was low, but every word was intensely distinct.

'Dick!' With a tremendous effort Moira recovered herself. 'It really is you?'

'Of course . . . ' Richard Lane took off his hat and revealed firmly-brushed dark hair and a good forehead. His face was lean and strong. There was a cold, deadly glint in his dark eyes.

'Wh-what are you doing here?' Moira stammered. 'My husband will be back with some coal at any moment . . . '

'No he won't,' Richard Lane said. 'I saw the light switched on in the basement, so I went and knocked on the outer door. He opened it.' Silence, then

Lane added, 'We shan't be disturbed, Sylvia — Moira — or whatever you call yourself.'

'What have you done to him?' Moira demanded sharply.

He did not answer. Turning to the window again he drew the drapes, then locked the door and removed the key.

'Why don't you admit that you're surprised?' he asked coldly. 'You've seen me three times in London and just missed me; now you see me again. Haven't you any comments?'

'Then it *was* you I saw?' she asked slowly, her venomous look darkening.

'Yes, it was, but I'll bet you couldn't understand it!'

Moira did not admit that he had spoken truth. She was still struggling to get a hold of herself and, at the same time, wondering what had happened to Perry.

'Y'know,' Richard Lane went on pensively, sitting on the arm of the chair and taking a cigarette from his case, 'it's all so pitifully easy when it's explained — Oh, have one?'

He held out the case casually. For answer Moira whipped out her hand and sent the case spinning across the room.

'Get out of here, Dick!' she breathed, her voice quivering. 'Go on — get out!'

'Such temper,' he reproved, going over to the case and picking it up. He returned to his perch on the chair and struck a match, and regarded the girl with cold eyes.

'Such temper indeed,' he added. 'You should learn to control it. However, as I was saying, it's all so easily explained. I was never in custody to start with. The law can't arrest an innocent person — or didn't you know that?'

Moira was breathing hard. 'What are you talking about?'

'You know what I'm talking about. If you want it more plainly, the game's up! You're only one jump ahead of a murder conviction, and I've enjoyed every minute of running you to earth, of helping the police and Dr. Castle — '

He was on his feet before Moira realized it. His hand shot out, caught her arm and whirled her to him. It was a grip that she could not break.

'When I told you, as any decent man would, that it wasn't fair of me to continue my attentions towards you because I was sick of your queer fads and foibles, and because I had fallen in love with Joyce Kempton, what did you do? You killed her? Murdered her — horribly — cut her throat in as vile an exhibition of jealous rage as any I ever witnessed!'

'You couldn't have known,' Moira said, her eyes dilated. 'you couldn't have! You couldn't have seen me — '

'But I did. Joyce's apartment house is one of those places where men are not allowed to visit the girl tenants. So Joyce and I had an arrangement. I used to go up the fire-escape — just as you must have done. I saw everything you did because I had just arrived to see Joyce and you were in the room with her. I didn't get away quickly enough, for as you left you saw me. I tried to seize you in that alley, but you got away . . . I should have told the police there and then, but I didn't because I remembered I'd told my landlady that I was going to see Joyce and knew just what the police would think. My only hope was to get hold of you, drag you to the police.'

20

Richard Lane flung her fiercely into the easy chair and stood glowering down upon her.

'You evaded me,' he went on, clenching his fists. 'You took a train to London. I followed. You plunged your suitcase into that jeweler's window and smashed it — purely, I think, for the sake of attracting attention and stopping me following you. Then you ran — until you met Lonsdale. But I kept on your trail.'

Richard Lane stopped. Moira remained just as he had thrown her, white fury in her face. When Lane spoke again, his voice had become a little quieter.

'I lost track of you when you went into the Barryvale hotel, and I was arrested. I told the police everything, but though they were satisfied with my story, they had not sufficient evidence to warrant arresting you. There were legal factors in the way, certain missing parts. I offered to help, determined to bring you to justice.'

'So?' Moira's voice was a whisper.

'I don't exactly know what arrangements the police made,' he answered. 'I was asked to appear at certain places at certain times, and everything was arranged for me by Scotland Yard. I let you see me for a moment in Chandos Street after a Yard man had seen you leave your flat. Then I disappeared in the crowd, according to instructions. You saw me again in the Silver Grill on which occasion two Yard people were with me as apparent friends. Again I disappeared.'

'Then after I fainted in the theater, it was somebody else who came up and called himself Gerald Cavendish,' Moira said fiercely. 'It was a trick — a dirty scheming trick! It was you in the stalls — '

'I left the theater,' Lane said. 'Perhaps another man who resembled me was used after that. I don't know. One other thing I did was write a note to you, after making a date for a meeting.'

'And did you meet me?' Moira snapped.

He shook his head. 'No . . . As for tonight, I came here with Chief Inspector Calthorp, Sergeant Dixon, Dr. Castle and a couple of constables. Perry is with them now. There's nothing you can do, Moira. They've got you!'

'I can hang for one murder,' she said slowly, her eyes glinting, 'but I may as well have my money's worth — '

In one bound she was on her feet and hurtled like a dark shadow across the room to the drinks cabinet. Seizing the whiskey decanter, she smashed it against the top edge of the cabinet. The glass shattered. With the half-neck clutched in her hand, she advanced slowly towards Richard Lane.

'So you'd work with the police against me, would you?' Her voice was hardly audible. 'I'm going to kill you for that, Dick! It's the only thing I have ever wanted to do since you threw me over for Joyce Kempton. I killed her, because she had taken you away from me. On the night I thought I was going to meet you in response to your note, I went all prepared with a tumbler. I was going to smash it in your neck! I even drugged my husband to stop him going with me and spoiling my plans. Something went wrong and you didn't meet me, but — ' Moira smiled crookedly — 'you are here now!'

Richard Lane remained motionless, watching her narrowly.

'I don't let anybody come between me and the person I love,' she went on, swinging the decanter-top gently as though it were a pendulum. 'When I married Perry, there was a girl who tried it — Helen Ransome. I'd have killed her, too, if she hadn't been too quick for me. I believe,' she added absently, 'I'd even kill Perry, too, now I seem to have lost him — '

Her momentary preoccupation lost her the advantage. Lane sprang forward, forced her arm up and back and the decanter top went flying into the shadows. He caught her roughly and forced her into a chair. She did not protest. She was suddenly crying bitterly.

A voice seemed to come to her from a long way off.

'Mrs. Lonsdale . . . ' Then as she tried

to think who could be speaking, it came again — sharply, commandingly: 'Mrs. Lonsdale!'

She glanced up and saw a gigantic figure looming against the glow of the tall reading lamp. Behind it, lesser figures waited, silent. Chief Inspector Calthorp, Sergeant Dixon and Perry.

'Mrs. Lonsdale,' Adam Castle said. 'I have something to say to you.'

'What do you want?' she muttered. 'I murdered Joyce Kempton, and I tried to murder Helen Ransome . . . I'd do it again in the same circumstances.'

'I know you would,' Adam Castle said quietly. 'Severe crystalophobia allied to an intensely jealous nature is a dangerous combination.'

Moira's dark eyes fixed on him in sullen fury. 'I don't know what you're talking about!'

'Yes, you do, Mrs. Lonsdale, otherwise you would never have bought those books on mental trouble in an effort to cure yourself. You know you hate glass in every shape and form, mirrors included.'

The girl was silent. The psychiatrist

drew up a chair and sat down so that his face was away from the light while Moira's was fully exposed to it.

'Just relax for a moment, Mrs. Lonsdale,' he murmured.

'I won't! I — '

'Yes you will,' Castle assured her. 'Close your eyes . . . ' He waited a moment. 'That's it. Breathe deeply — slowly — gently. Now again. Very gently.'

To the assembled men the shadowy room seemed to crawl with the psychiatrist's soothing words.

'If you can hear me, Mrs. Lonsdale, just answer yes.'

'Yes.'

'Good . . . It is a bright, sunny day. You are feeling extremely happy because you are going on a picnic. Your father is at the wheel of the car and your mother is in the seat beside him. You are seated next to your mother. You are six-year-old Sylvia Cotswood going for a day's outing to Reading. That is right, is it not?'

'Yes, we are going to Reading for a picnic,' Moira repeated mechanically.

'The car is a new one. Your father has a reckless nature and drives too fast. There is a truck ahead. You father can't stop the car! There is a terrific smashing of glass and a piece of the windshield tears across the throat of your mother and just misses you — '

'*Stop it!*' Moira screamed. 'Stop it! I can't stand it!'

Silence. The fire, bereft of coal, slipped into a glowing ash.

'All right, Mrs. Lonsdale,' Castle said quietly, taking her arm. 'That's all.'

He helped her to her feet, then stooping, he picked up the shattered half of the decanter and handed it to her.

'What would you like to do with this?' he asked.

'Nothing,' she answered shakenly. 'It — it doesn't seem to mean anything any more — Oh, Dr. Castle, if only I had known you years ago . . .'

'The fact remains,' the chief inspector said curtly, 'that murder has been done, and you, Mrs. Lonsdale, are under arrest.'

★ ★ ★

233

Three days later Perry received a letter from Dr. Castle, It read:

'My dear Lonsdale:

'Since you will, of course, have to attend the trial of your wife, I feel that a clearing up of one or two factors is due in advance — to you especially — so herewith I state them. First and foremost, in regard to your wife, please understand that the terrible car accident in which, as a child, she was involved was the direct underlying cause of her actions — that, and a naturally jealous nature.

'My meeting with your wife and yourself was deliberately arranged — you heard Richard Lane explain as the four of us listened outside the drawing-room door on the evening of your wife's arrest how he, too, helped Scotland Yard. Incidentally, another man was substituted for him at the theater. The reason for this Lane 'subterfuge' I'll make clear in a moment . . .

'Calthorp's trouble, despite material

evidence that your wife was the culprit was lack of motive for her act. Why for instance, had she used a smashed bottle of eau-de-cologne when there was a pair of scissors lying handy? When he consulted me he had already interviewed and released Richard Lane, and seen your wife. It puzzled him that your wife had referred to Lane's phobia regarding glass, a fact to which Lane himself had never alluded. It occurred to me then that we were perhaps tackling a mind working inversely — in other words the kind of mind which makes its own faults seem to belong to somebody else. It is a defensive screen that some people set up, especially neurotics . . . If this were so, the very fact of your wife mentioning it and Lane not doing so might suggest that she was the key to the problem.

'Satisfied in my own mind that she and not Lane was the crystalophobia sufferer, I had to decide the possible motive. The only likely one seemed to be jealousy (which gave me my foothold for building up the electra complex). First, Joyce Kempton had come between her and Lane, and to add point to the jealousy angle Moira used the very bottle of eau-de-cologne which Lane had given Joyce as a present (he admitted this in his police statement). Second, Helen Ransome had made no effort to disguise her affection for you and had given you a pair of decanters for your wedding present. The similarity between the attack on Joyce and that on Helen left no doubts in my mind. Further, nobody else but Moira could have drugged that coffee.

'In regard to this latter, Moira was clever. She drugged yours when she poured it out, but she only took her own after committing the crime. She knew that by the time the drug had taken effect the law would have arrived and she would be pronounced genuinely unconscious. Incidentally, Helen mentioned the strong grip of her attacker; this was amply borne out when your wife, emotionally disturbed by holding a wine glass, snapped the stem of it in her hand. (Needless to relate, Moira took full advantage of Helen's resemblance to her to work out a really neat 'red herring' which put the blame on Richard. She didn't see Richard through that window and she didn't really faint. It was a clever build-up to pin Helen's intended fate on Richard.)

'I had next to decide whether it was just hatred of her own sex or sheer jealousy with no sex-angle involved at all. I arranged with the Yard for a note to be sent by Richard Lane. According to my calculations, if Moira were anxious to kill Lane (because he had thrown her over), she would probably use glass as her weapon. I was right. A Yard man was waiting for her and robbed her of the tumbler. It satisfied me that she hated Lane where once she had loved him.

'Sure of my ground as to motive and method of weapon used, I had to soften her up in readiness for the time when she would, from sheer emotional crisis break down and confess. I contrived (with the Yard's connivance) three mysterious appearances of Lane. This, as I had planned, had a disastrous effect on her self-control and when she really did meet Lane she reacted as I had hoped and admitted everything, even trying again to kill him — again with glass. Naturally, both you and she were watched all the time. Her whole story of pursuing Lane was a fabrication: he was pursuing her . . .

'So, Lonsdale, I have done my best to give you an advance report. If there is anything that is not clear to you, don't hesitate to call on me and we'll discuss it.

'Believe me to be your sincere friend.
'ADAM CASTLE.'

Perry lowered the letter and smiled ruefully. As far as he could tell there was no point that was not clear to him — so he did not see the psychiatrist again until the court proceedings. The verdict was 'Guilty — but insane.'

We do hope that you have enjoyed reading this large print book.

Did you know that all of our titles are available for purchase?

We publish a wide range of high quality large print books including:

Romances, Mysteries, Classics
General Fiction
Non Fiction and Westerns

Special interest titles available in large print are:

The Little Oxford Dictionary
Music Book, Song Book
Hymn Book, Service Book

Also available from us courtesy of Oxford University Press:

Young Readers' Dictionary
(large print edition)
Young Readers' Thesaurus
(large print edition)

For further information or a free brochure, please contact us at:
Ulverscroft Large Print Books Ltd.,
The Green, Bradgate Road, Anstey,
Leicester, LE7 7FU, England.
Tel: (00 44) **0116 236 4325**
Fax: (00 44) **0116 234 0205**

REFLECTED GLORY

John Russell Fearn

When artist Clive Hexley, R. A.
vanishes, Chief Inspector Calthorp of
Scotland Yard is called upon to look
into the disappearance, and his
investigations lead him to question
Hexley's ex-fiancée, Elsa Farraday.
Elsa confesses that she has murdered
the artist. The girl's peculiar manner
puzzles Calthorp, and he hesitates to
make an arrest, particularly as
Hexley's body cannot be found. It is
not until Calthorp calls in Dr. Adam
Castle, the psychiatrist investigator,
that the strange mystery of Elsa's
behaviour and the artist's disappearance is solved.

A HEARSE FOR McNALLY

G. J. Barrett

Gerry Westmayne had worked out how to steal the State Jewels of Lahkpore. McNally carried out the plan but, with cracksman Herb Setters, he stole the loot from Westmayne's safe only to discover that it was worthless. McNally had been outsmarted, and he began to wonder if he could trust Gilda Kemp. And after killing his boss he realized the extent of his girlfriend's treachery and learned too late the high cost of a place in the sun.

POISON IN THE BLOOD

Patrick Dolan

Peter Low (alias Jack Johnson) may not be the first released prisoner to feel poison towards society. But few face the problem of finding their girl married to a man with the mind of a child. Add two more characters, one dumb and one razor sharp but both ruthless. Switch the scenes between the lonely farmhouse they are converting for the child and his beautiful wife, and a series of daring robberies, and suspense mounts. But no 'nice' ending is possible in this absorbing story.